WITHOUT A DOUBT

A SMALL TOWN ISLAND ROMANCE

STONE'S THROW ISLAND

PARKER ROSE

Copyright © 2022 by Parker Rose

All rights reserved.

No part of this book may be reproduced in any form or by any electronic or mechanical means, including information storage and retrieval systems, without written permission from the author, except for the use of brief quotations in a book review.

To request permissions, contact the author at parkerrose@stonesthrowisland.com

Paperback ISBN: 978-1-959516-00-2
Ebook ISBN: 978-1-959516-01-9

First paperback edition October 2022

Edited by Heather Kelly
Cover art by Lisa Messegee

Rocky Points Press
Massachusetts
USA

www.stonesthrowisland.com

*For anyone who follows their true north
(or Magic Eight Ball).*

1

I had never been to the island alone. The wind blew cold spray across the bow of the ferry and I pulled my unlined, plastic raincoat as far around me as I could. I stood in the mist, clutching the metal guardrail in my gloved hands, steeling myself against the rolling of the boat. In every direction, there was only sea and fog. Occasionally a seagull dipped low enough to the boat that I could see it—that was the only sign that we were close to the shore and not cruising aimlessly in the middle of the ocean.

"I can't believe I'm doing this," I muttered, and then looked quickly around. The deck was empty; nobody within earshot to hear me talk to myself like a crazy person. Everyone else had taken shelter from the rainy weather in the cabin behind me.

I resisted the urge to ask my Magic Eight Ball keychain if I should be doing this by myself. The levity that app brought to marketing meetings and my normal life seemed out of place on the journey to Stone's Throw Island to settle my aunt's affairs.

Mist turned into actual rain and I tucked my head even farther back into my hood. Coming to this island at the beginning of spring certainly wasn't my idea. Being on the island was going to serve as a reality check that my aunt Del was really gone. It was my first time back since she passed and I expected to feel her presence everywhere. This was going to be rough.

Why would she leave me her house in the will? I had assumed all her assets would go to my mom or her other sister, my aunt Sally. Or her girlfriend, Sylvi. As soon as work had settled down a bit, I had taken time off to take this trip, settle my aunt's affairs, and sell her island home.

My phone buzzed, and I ignored the urge to look. I hadn't taken a real vacation from my marketing job for years; they could let me have this one uninterrupted break. Some vacation—I was already wet and cold, even before reaching the island. And yet, I smiled into the churning water below. There was something fun about riding a ferry in bad weather, especially since everyone else had gone inside the little cabin and I was alone. Plus, it felt like the right atmosphere to return to the island in the wake of my aunt's death. Alone with the sea. Alone with my thoughts. Alone with ... my buzzing phone.

"Yes?" I resisted the impulse to throw the phone into the rolling waves. The moment I heard the question from my coworker on the other end of the phone, the scene in front of me disappeared. I turned around so my back sheltered the phone from the wind and dug into the conversation.

"You'll miss the best part." An elderly man joined me on the bow, and I could barely hear his choppy sentence before the wind blew it out over the choppy sea.

I ignored him and continued my work call, scrunching up my nose at the stranger. Was I being rude, or was he? Like most things in life, the answer was probably somewhere in the middle.

"The lighthouse will appear out of nowhere. It's the best when it's foggy like this."

Was he still talking to me? I excused myself from the call after promising my assistant, Sheila, that I would find Wi-Fi and make the desired client changes as soon as I landed safely on the island.

"If you let gadgets run your life, you'll miss out on the good stuff."

I shoved my phone back into my pocket, hoping the rain wouldn't seep into its insides and destroy it, and turned back to the bow of the boat, for the first time checking out the old guy insistent on having this conversation. He was dressed for the weather, decked out in a blue raincoat, most likely lined with some cozy material, and rain hat. His face was kind and open.

"What's the good stuff?" This should be something.

"The island will suddenly appear, like Brigadoon. Like it's not quite real."

"But it is real, right?" The old guy was right—being on a boat in the middle of the ocean shrouded in fog with waves splashing mist into my hair and rain sprinkling down felt oddly surreal.

"Oh, it's real. And the good stuff is this moment. Being inside this moment. The smell of salt, the cold of the ocean mist, the warmth of the rain, and …" He paused for a long moment, so long I wondered if he would ever finish the sentence. My hand itched to take my phone out and surf the web for comparison ads I could model for my client who wanted the change. Hmmm. Maybe it wasn't just my assistant who couldn't allow me to unplug and have a "vacation."

A low guttural horn wailed somewhere.

"… the sound of the foghorn. I've always wondered why the sound calling us home would sound so lost. The good stuff." The guy looked eagerly out into the sea.

"It's not calling me home."

The man looked at me expectantly, but I didn't offer up any more of an explanation. No need to open up to a stranger. No need to open up to anyone here, at all. I'd take care of things and get back to my real life as soon as possible. Especially since I had gone through two big breakups recently, in part because of my tendency to jump in and throw my whole self into situations. Matt and I had parted friends, but it still hurt. Frank was a different story altogether. So now, I pledged to not let myself jump into this adventure. I'd just do the work and get back to my own life.

The foghorn wailed again, startling me out of my reverie, and I looked expectantly off the bow of the ferry.

A ghost island rose up in front of us just as the man had said it would. Rocky shoreline and a sweeping beach, with a beacon lighthouse to the side. A shiver danced up my spine. The warm glow of the lighthouse beam pulled the boat to shore like a magnet. Unexpectedly, and for the first time in a long time, I felt I was exactly where I should be. I pushed my hand into my pocket and pressed the off button on my phone.

"I'm Jack." The man extended his hand in greeting.

"Paige." I shook his hand.

"Have a good day, Paige." The man went back into the warmth of the cabin. I stayed out on the deck watching the island fill in with color and detail as we got closer and closer until the boat reversed and softly bumped to a stop at the pier. I waited until the line of ferry riders subsided, and then pulled my rolling suitcase down the ramp and out onto the dock.

"I hope the island reveals its magic to you, Paige." Jack managed the last step from the ramp onto the wood of the pier like a man half his age. "Every-day magic is the hardest to find. But if you are still enough, open enough, and willing enough, it's the best gift you can receive."

"I'm not staying long." I slowed my stride to match Jack's. As much as I decided not to get involved on a personal level, I wasn't about to be rude.

"Vacation?"

"Not really. Do you know where I can rent a car?" Normally I booked all these details in advance, but for some odd reason, I hadn't found a single online car rental place on the island when I planned the trip. Aunt Del had always welcomed me on the pier with an extra bike, and that's how we got around.

We stepped off the pier and onto a sidewalk, past a parking lot, and toward the Main Street, lined with a cute row of shops, restaurants, and old-fashioned hotels facing the ferry dock and beaches. The buildings rose out of the fog in a friendly sort of way.

Jack enthusiastically spoke up. "No cars to rent on the island. In fact, very few cars at all. There's a rule. Safer for everyone."

"Wow, that's backward-thinking," I said before I could filter. I knew I sounded elitist. But no cars? How would I get to my aunt's house? And it put into perspective all those times I had visited and she had that extra bike ready to go. Aunt Del had been all about fitness and healthy living, I had never thought it anything except a quirk of her personality. Not a quirk of the whole island.

"We just really like the way things are on the island. We're not against change; it just needs to be a good change. Most people use mopeds. Or bikes."

I closed my eyes. Brought back to all those adventures I had with Aunt Del. Being on this island without her was going to be a special sort of torture. Best to pack up her house and settle her affairs as quickly as possible.

"Well, I can't very well put my suitcase on a moped."

"Oh, but you can. There's a spot you can strap it down."

This was turning out to be more of an adventure than I had bargained for. An adventure I didn't want.

Jack pointed out a moped rental place, across the street, and quickly said goodbye. The rain was really driving now.

I hurriedly stepped into the street.

A large truck honked its horn, slammed on its brakes, and slid sideways toward me on the slick street. I jumped back to the sidewalk as it careened toward me, tripping over the curb and landing in a deep puddle. The truck came to a teetering stop inches from the bottom of my rain boots.

"What the hell are you thinking?!" The guy in the truck opened his door and jumped out because almost killing me clearly wasn't enough; he needed to yell at me too.

I breathed hard, feeling the cold puddle seep into my clothes. At least I wouldn't have to apply ice to my bruising backside. This was just perfect. A cold, miserable, painful start to what was going to be a sad, miserable week of cleaning out and selling my beloved aunt's house.

"I was thinking there were no trucks on this god-forsaken island!?"

He leaned down and held out his hand. I pushed aside my feelings of personal woe and noticed that he was actually really good-looking. Brown hair glistening in the rain, brown piercing eyes, and bulging arm muscles.

"I don't need help." I un-gracefully pulled myself out of the puddle and tried to smooth the water out of my pants. I was freezing. And now I understood the difference between water-resistant and water-proof. My upscale Boston wardrobe wasn't holding up to wet island spring adventures. I was soaked everywhere, including beneath my so-called rain jacket. Luckily my phone was in my pocket and not broken on the street. I tapped the lump it made against my thigh, hoping it was still functional.

"We have some vehicles for emergency response, like this one, and a few others around the island."

"You're supposed to respond to emergencies, not create them, right?" Why was I standing in the rain, arguing with this guy? I hedged toward the moped place, this time looking both ways as I stepped off the curb.

"And you're supposed to look both ways before stepping into the street."

"I DIDN'T THINK THERE WERE ANY CARS HERE." I jogged over to the moped place, my suitcase bouncing erratically behind me, hurting my wrist, as I tried to keep it upright and on its wheels.

He followed me into the moped place. Why, was beyond me.

I walked into the tiny rental shop and shook off the rain. A girl my age sat behind the counter, swiping on an iPad. Thank goodness, a sign of real-world technology. Before I could even open my mouth to speak, the guy who nearly ended my life took over.

"Look, the least I can do is give you a ride to wherever you need to go."

"No, the least you can do is *nothing*. And that's what I'd prefer you do." I was literally shivering and just wanted this whole day to be over.

The guy looked me up and down. I wondered what I looked like. Mascara running, lips pursed like a petulant child, eyes shooting daggers. Whatever he saw, it made him change his tact.

"Hey, Henri, can you give her a deal on a moped rental?"

Henri, the very pretty girl behind the counter, with dual braids hanging down her shirt, would have to wait. I turned to the guy behind me, noticing how his brown eyes seemed concerned and kind. Still, no reason for him to butt in. As if I was a feeble person who couldn't do this on my own.

"I can do this on my own, you know." I put both hands up in the universal gesture of, I-got-this-so-back-off-guy-with-bulging-arms-wearing-only-a-t-shirt-even-though-it-was-miserable-outside. I ignored that he had already asked the question, and leaned onto the thin counter to talk conspiratorially with Henri.

"Henri, I would love to rent a moped. One that hopefully has a place for my suitcase."

"Sure."

Henri pushed some paperwork toward me. "Have you ever ridden a moped before?"

"Nope."

She nodded. "It's not difficult. You'll get the hang of it quickly. Pretty much like driving a car without the car around you. Or riding a fast bike, actually." She paused to consider exactly what riding a moped was like, and then shrugged. "I'll help you strap down the suitcase so it's balanced on the back."

I perused the contract and signed it in all the right places. Well, tried to sign it. Even my fingers were shaking from the cold.

"Maybe I should just give you a ride." He was still there, behind me. "Where are you going? You're not dressed for this weather."

As if *he* was dressed for this weather. I sighed. Maybe if I just ignored him, he'd go away. I pushed my credit card across the counter to Henri. "I'm sure I can figure out how to strap my suitcase down."

"You out on an emergency call, Jesse?"

The guy edged in beside me in the tiny office. "A call. Not an emergency really, but yup. A tree is down across Coastal Ave."

Henri nodded, sliding a set of keys to me. "Suit yourself…" She checked the name on the contract. "… Paige. It's the blue one out front." Henri pointed to a row of mopeds I could barely see through the driving rain. A blue moped capped the end of the row.

She returned my card, and I pulled my suitcase back to the door, wondering how wet my packed clothes were going to get inside the suitcase while I drove to my aunt's place. It's possible I would get there and not have anything dry at all. My heart skipped a beat as I thought of my work laptop nestled in the middle of my clothes. I pushed the worry aside; nothing I could do now except hope that the water didn't seep all the way in.

"See you, Jesse." Henri turned back to her iPad. "Jesse" followed me outside. I used the bungees attached to the bike to secure the suitcase to the back of the moped and then sat astride it, plugging my aunt's address into my phone. It was slow going; my phone's screen wasn't a fan of being wet. I was glad it was still functioning at all.

"Why don't you let me throw the moped into the back of my truck. You can warm up in my cab as I take you where you need to go. The bed and breakfast? A hotel? The Meadowlark Inn? Where are you staying?"

"As if I'm going to tell a complete stranger, who almost ran me down with his truck on an island that is not supposed to have trucks, where I'm staying." I still couldn't get the directions up on my phone, but like hell was I going to stay here with this strange, if cute, guy.

I turned the key on the moped. The plastic floatie on the keychain dangled low, letting me know that if I accidentally rode the moped into the ocean, the key wouldn't be lost forever. There was a pretty good chance of me riding this sucker into the ocean since I didn't know the island and didn't know where I was going. And I certainly didn't know how to ride a moped. But all I wanted to do was get away from the prying eyes of this stranger.

None too gracefully, I drove the thing out of the parking lot and down the main street, imagining Jesse's eyes on my butt the whole way. Even feeling so self-conscious, and trying not to crash, I noticed the cutest little shops and businesses along the left-hand side of the main drag, with a gorgeous view of a crescent moon-shaped beach on the right.

I drove around the corner, feeling foolish. I had no idea if I was even going in the right direction. As soon as I was certain I was out of sight, I pulled off the road and onto the sandy shoulder. I held my phone under the cover of my own body and tried to plug in the address again. It took several tries before I finally typed the address correctly into the wet screen. I said a strong prayer to the phone gods: *Please don't let my phone get so waterlogged it stops working!* Clearly, if I had anything emergency-adjacent, the island people would send Jesse my way.

Luckily the directions to my aunt's place didn't include me banging a U-turn and driving back into town. I memorized the way as best I could and zipped the phone into my jacket pocket. Getting the moped out of the wet sandy shoulder was harder than I thought. I finally got off the damn thing and pushed it. Praying to different gods, maybe the embarrassment gods: *Please don't let Jesse come this way and see me pushing the moped out of this quicksand!*

I made it the rest of the way to my aunt's house without incident. I had to stop one more time to check directions, but I wasn't foolish enough to pull off the road again. When I arrived, I threw both hands into the air in celebration. I did it. Which seemed a little ridiculous, considering that I made million-dollar marketing deals on a monthly basis, and here I was feeling triumphant that I had driven a mile down the road on a moped in the rain.

I wrestled my suitcase up the steps to the wrap-around porch and grabbed the key from inside the conch shell decoratively placed in the basket next to the door. Just as the lawyer said it would be.

Inside, the house was still and quiet. I peeled off my raincoat and hung it at the umbrella/coat stand next to the door. Shivering, but ignoring my wrinkled hands and the desire to jump in a hot shower and just stand there for as much time as it took to forget the falling-in-the-puddle-incident, I turned the heat up. From the front door, I could see all the way through the house and to the picture windows in the back, overlooking what my aunt had always lovingly called the bog. The fog was still so thick, that the backyard was just a cloudy mystery.

I wandered through the downstairs, with the feeling that my aunt would pop out from around some corner. I didn't realize how much I still missed her until right this second. I thought I had said my goodbyes at the funeral, but I guess you never really set the sadness all the way aside when someone close to you dies.

Being in her home without her hit me hard. She had been a special beacon in my life, showing me how to be a successful career woman. She had been a doctor and so good at her job, that I had been confused when she moved full-time into what had once been her vacation home. I mean, sure there was a small hospital on the island, but she could have impacted so many more lives on the mainland.

And clearly, our relationship had meant more to her than I had ever known since she left the place to me. She always treated me so special, but she had a way of treating everyone that way. Bittersweet. That was what this feeling was—so happy our relationship had meant as much to her as it did me, but sad I hadn't made more of an effort to spend time with her. Come to the island more often. Was a ferry ride really too much trouble to make the trip?

I pushed the guilt aside and ran my hands over a shelf of books. Walked into the cheery kitchen, and checked the fridge for something to eat. Someone had already removed all the perishables that would have gone bad between her death and the time I could push things around in my work life to come out to settle her affairs.

That was kind. Probably Sylvi. I wished she were here to help me, but my aunt's girlfriend had told me that everything on the island reminded her of Del. She was trying to get a hold on her grief by spending time on the mainland with her nephew and his new baby. It sounded like she didn't know if she'd come back to the island at all.

I sighed.

In the front of the fridge sat a full bottle of white wine, chilling. In a moment of nostalgia, I poured two glasses.

Raising my glass, and feeling more alone than I ever had before, I spoke aloud. "I miss you, Aunt Del."

Unwanted tears streamed down my face. I gulped down the wine. A hot shower could not be put off any longer. Everything else could wait. I lifted my glass up in another toast. "I wish I had known how much I would miss you before you left." I navigated the stairs slowly, wine in one hand, suitcase in another, tears streaming down my face.

2

The wind howled through the bog, and weird scratching noises seemed to be everywhere all at once. Rain pelted the roof above me. I stared at the ceiling fan in my aunt's bedroom and considered pulling a pillow over my head. Sleep was always hard the first night in a strange bed, but this was ridiculous. At least I was warm and cozy, finally. I flipped my smartwatch over and its glowing face told me it was three am. If I couldn't sleep, maybe I should get up and get working.

I had planned on hitting the ground running by boxing up everything in the house in the next few days—but being exhausted from no sleep was really going to make everything so much harder. The driving rain sounded so close it might have been inside the room with me.

CRASH.

The house shook. Something had hit the roof. I sat up, wide-awake now.

It's okay, this house is built for weather. But the thought wasn't comforting. At all.

What if there was someone in the house?

I grabbed my phone to use as a flashlight and jumped out of

bed. There was no one else but her to investigate. *Pull up your big-girl panties, Paige.*

I was groggy and not thinking straight, which probably meant I had fallen asleep without realizing it or that I had drunk the whole bottle of wine myself. (Or both.) Because, really, I didn't need a flashlight, I could just turn on all the lights. Which I did. I flicked on every lamp and light switch within reach, as I hunted down what might have caused the bang. Good thing too, since the flashlight went dead, signaling the death of my cell phone. I sighed into the storm sounds beating the house.

"Nice, Paige. You didn't have to go back down and drink Aunt Del's glass of wine ... and the entire bottle. And then forget to do the important stuff, like plug in your goddamn phone." I thought speaking aloud would make me feel better, but my voice just sounded tired, tiny, and alone in the house. Punctuating how far from my real life and the real world I was. Alone.

I had wanted to be in charge of my own destiny. And here I was, by myself on a stormy island with no phone to call for help if a stranger was in the house right now, waiting behind the next corner to murder me with an ax.

Would they use an ax? I considered the murdering tools available on an island. An oar? That would probably be too heavy to carry to the murder site. A knife to scale fish? That had an ominous ring to it. Pummeled by a life vest? I giggled in spite of myself.

By this point in my murder musings, I slipped back into the kitchen, the house blazing with as much light as an old Victorian could. The giant windows showcased the storm outside, lit by the floodlights I had turned on in my flip-every-switch mode.

It was like a movie set, with the sound turned way up. Rain battered the house. Lightning flashed across the bog. A fog horn howled in the distance. It was impossible to not feel a little exhilarated. And then two things happened simultaneously. Something crashed through the kitchen's bay windows shattering all the glass, and all the lights went out.

I screamed, jumped, and collapsed to the ground next to the sink. The storm was suddenly inside the house for real.

Huddled on the ground, I tried to get my bearings. Wind and rain whipped at my skimpy sleep shirt and shorts. I touched my face to see if the glass had hit me. I seemed okay. I pushed the on-button on my phone, praying to the tech gods that they would send some miracle juice to the phone battery. No such luck.

Don't be stupid, Paige. If it was a murderer, you'd be dead already. It must have been a tree branch. If you die right now it's because you're sitting underneath another window in a storm, waiting for a second tree to fall on you. MOVE!

But I couldn't. I wanted to cry. Why had I come here?

"Big girl panties, Paige. Big girl panties. Nobody is going to save you but yourself, and that's the way you want it, right?" My voice sounded pitiful even to myself.

I took another stab at the pep talk. "Get UP. Paige, it's only rain. And trees. And lightning," I said as the lightning crashed and illuminated the scariest-looking tree lying across the eat-in breakfast-nook table.

Avoiding mucky leaves, glass, and tree debris, I half crawled, half ran into the relative safety of the library, and huddled in the corner on the oriental rug. I waited for my heart to stop pounding like it wanted to leave my chest. *Breathe. Breathe.*

"For the love of Pete, it's only a TREE!" I started to count down from one hundred to calm myself, but that only reminded me of that scene in Poltergeist when they were counting between the lightning flashes and thunder and that scared me even more. No counting, then.

By the light of the next lightning flash, I could see the room, just as my aunt left it. A cozy library den. I felt her presence suddenly. The few times I had visited, we had joyful, happy, laughing moments in this room. Talking about her work at the hospital, about my ad campaigns like the one for my company's cosmetic client: Lipstick, not just for ladies anymore! Thunder derailed my thoughts. But I picked them up again when the thunder stopped for a moment, and I sank against the solid rock around the fireplace. Happy memories of my aunt allowed me to think straight again.

"Okay, Paige, the electricity is not going to magically go back on. You need to get up, get dressed, find a flashlight, and get the tree out of the kitchen. Your aunt left you to take care of her house and that's what you're gonna do." My voice was stronger now, and I started to believe myself. "You can do this, Paige." I shivered. Soaked again, for the second time in less than twenty-four hours on this island.

Okay. Flashlight first. If I were Aunt Del, where would I keep a flashlight? Thunder rolled and lightning flashed through the house. "Everywhere." If I lived here, I'd keep flashlights everywhere. And have a generator. Why didn't my aunt install a generator?! "Stop being a wuss."

Aunt Del was pragmatic. She'd keep flashlights in the kitchen and near the front door, right? No way in hell was I going back into the stormy kitchen, so ... I wanted to walk calmly to the front hall closet—to show this storm who was boss—but all I could manage was a crab-like crawl, against the walls in case something else exploded through a window. If an island in the middle of the ocean had one thing to teach me, it was that I wasn't the boss. Nature was.

I opened the giant hall closet and ran my hands along the shelves inside. Baskets of batteries, hats, frisbees, and other paraphernalia. Finally, my fingers stumbled onto an organized array of flashlights, and (thank the rain gods!) fake candles. I switched on several flashlights and several fake candles which immediately made the night seem fun instead of scary. A blast back to the past, to a time when candles were lamps.

Thunder boomed nearby and the fun died a quick death. I skittered away, upstairs, hoping that another tree didn't fall on the top of the house while I was up there. I stripped off the wet clothes and left them wherever they fell. Ransacked my own suitcase, pushing aside all the clothes that were already damp or that weren't storm-worthy.

The tiny eight ball keychain my friend Cynthia had given me as a joke, but which I actually used all the time, rolled across the room. Most of my clothes littered the floor before I found some heavy sweats, a long-sleeved shirt, and (I thanked my past self for packing SOMETHING pragmatic) a wool sweater. Itchy, yes. But warm. And, wool socks. With warm feet, I felt like a new woman. Trapped in a horror movie, maybe, but finally ready to become the heroine.

Lightning lit up the room as I shoved my hair back into a quick bun, grabbed the flashlight, and left a faux candle beside the bed. Future Paige would thank me for that. Staying away from windows, I ran downstairs.

I surveyed the fallen tree from the safety of the library. It wasn't a tree, after all, just a huge branch. The wind whipped the hair that escaped my bun. I needed to get the tree branch and storm back where it belonged—outside of my aunt's house.

Or, and this seemed much more appealing, I could let the storm rage and take care of it all in the light of day. *Big girl panties, Paige. Big girl panties.* If I waited until morning, who knew what kind of damage the rain would wreak on my aunt's house? She had loved this house. And had put it in my care. I needed to step up. "Okay, Aunt Del, what would you do?"

The answer seemed clear to me. She'd get that branch out of her house and somehow block the rain from coming inside.

Okay, then. I walked swiftly, determined now, feeling the cold metal flashlight as a talisman in my hand. Back to the front closet. I ignored my still-wet, weather-resistant parka on the coat rack, and pilfered my aunt's stuff. Found a quintessential island yellow, flannel-lined raincoat and pulled it on. I pulled the soft rubber-like hood over my head. Definitely weather-proof. I pulled on her knee-high wellies. Slightly too big, but they'd stay on my feet. Concerned I couldn't get through the kitchen to the back door because of the tree blocking the way, I stepped out the front door and into the wild wind of the storm.

The wind blew the hood off my head and my hair was

instantly soaked. I didn't worry about pulling the hood back up, but now I knew why my aunt always wore a rain hat with this jacket. Wrapping memories of my aunt around me like a bulletproof vest, I ran around the porch to the back. My light bobbed as I tried to keep my footing on the slick wood. The backyard was completely black and my flashlight only made a small dent in the dark. The tree limb was long. So long, that it reached all the way off the porch onto the sloped lawn toward the bog. The bog looked dark and menacing in the night.

Finally reaching the branch, I tugged at it, hoping it would just slide right out of the gaping window. No such luck. Maybe if I pulled from the lawn? I backtracked down the length of the house to the stairs leading to the backyard and held the banister securely as I climbed down the steps, slipping and sliding when I reached the wet grass.

As soon as I stepped onto the lawn, my right boot sucked down into the mud. Lawn was an overstatement—grass-lined muck was more apt. It was slow going as I used my cold, wet fingers to free each boot with every step. Juggling the heavy flashlight all the way to the tree branch. It looked smaller at this angle. I could totally pull it free. No problem.

I slowed my steps and my feet skimmed their way around rocks and small branches. Finally I found a large gap between branches at the base and gave it a tug. Lightning blazed and thunder crashed around me, so I huddled into the tree branch for some sort of safety.

I put the flashlight on the ground where it angled up at the base of the branch. I grabbed the branches at the bottom and squared myself off. *Please, whatever storm gods are looking down at me, please let this branch move when I pull on it.* Taking a deep breath, I bent my knees and pulled with all my might.

The only thing that moved was me. The tree stayed put and my boots stayed put. My hands slipped from the branches, and I fell backward down the incline, landing bootless, on my back. My head cracked hard on something solid and pain shot down my back.

I lay there, in the darkness, staring up at the nothingness. Wet, cold, getting wetter and colder every moment, and knowing with certainty that the storm gods were laughing down at me.

3

My head pounded in pain. Instead of getting up, I felt like yelling into the storm. So, I did. "Stupid storm. Stupid universe. Frank cheated on me, my aunt died, Matt moved across the country for a teaching gig, and now I can't seem to do anything right. How can I get my life back on track when everything is so hard?" I raged into the storm beating down on me. Tears streamed from my eyes as I let out all my fury.

Letting out my fury hurt my head.

"What are you doing here? Why are you at Delilah's house?"

A bright light blinded me. I wondered if this was what people talked about when they died. Well, at least I would see my aunt again soon.

The light moved aside and I stared up at a face while my heart sank even further. It was that guy from earlier. Jesse. The guy who almost killed me with his truck in the street. Of course. I could almost hear the storm gods laughing.

"Delilah's my, well she was, I mean. I'm her niece." Why was I explaining this to this rude guy? Who again stood over me while I lay in the rain.

"You're Del's niece?" His flashlight threw enough light on him that I could see him run his fingers through his hair with a thoughtful expression on his face, like he hadn't considered Aunt Delilah had family, let alone a niece. Then he seemed to realize that I was still lying in the mud. "Are you okay?" He held out his hand.

"I don't need your help." But I kinda did. My head was lower than my feet and I was tired and my head was pounding and there was a tree in my aunt's house.

I grabbed his hand and let him pull me up. I slid my feet back into boots and hoped he couldn't tell I was crying. Everything was wet and dark, so how could he? I swayed on my feet, dizzy and disoriented.

"Whoa, there." He held me to his chest to keep me up on my feet. I told myself I shouldn't—Frank had taught me the dangers of letting a guy help. I didn't know this guy at all. Not that knowing a guy meant that he wouldn't be controlling and cheat on you.

I shook my head, trying to focus on the here and now. Which just made me head hurt more. I winced. To be honest, I didn't know if I could get back to the house on my own two feet. And I felt warm and safe so close to him, in spite of the wet jackets between us. I ignored my internal warning signals and laid my head on his shoulder.

"Let's get you inside." He half-carried me to match his long strides.

"Thank you." My voice was quiet and got lost in the storm. All I wanted was someone else to fix everything—I was done with the struggles of the night. I knew I should rally and be strong, but all I thought I could actually do was sit down to try and stop my head from pounding.

"No problem, it's my job. Normally, anyway. I'm not on call tonight. I came by to check on Del's house in the storm. I saw your flashlight as I drove by. Thought someone was breaking in."

I let him rattle on, half-listening and not really caring. My head pulsed with every step. By the time we hit the stairs, I was feeling a little more in control of my legs, so I walked up them myself.

But he held on tight until we got inside and I settled into a chair in the den.

"Are you injured?" He kept his flashlight panned on me, but lower so as to not blind me. Again.

"I think I hit my head." I reached and pressed on the knot on the back of my scalp. *Ow.*

His hands gingerly felt the back of my skull until our fingers touched. I realized how close his body was to mine and my body reacted, shooting electricity into my stomach, against my head's wishes. It was nice to be distracted from the weirdness of the night. From the cold and pain. His fingers gently explored the bump.

"You'll live!" He cheerfully announced. As if in response to his proclamation, lights blazed on around us. "Well, that was quick—the power could be out for days on the island following a storm." He clicked off his flashlight. Where had my aunt's flashlight gone? I must have dropped it outside.

"You look like a drowned rat." He stepped back and surveyed me.

"Jeez, thanks." I held my throbbing head in my hands. I could see his feet inch closer as he inspected the back of my head in the light.

"You definitely whacked your head good on something. I don't think you need stitches. I'd love to wash away the ... mud ... just to make sure."

I touched the back of my head again and felt the matted hair, decorated with leaves and one small twig. "Ugh." The wind whipped through the house. Light or no, there was still a broken window and storm coming in.

"Let's get you out of these wet clothes and into a shower." He turned around. "Is EVERY light on in the house?"

"Yes. Every light I could find." It wasn't like he deserved an explanation. He was a stranger in my aunt's house. My head pulsed.

He disappeared for a moment and then returned and shoved a

glass of water in my hand. And a couple of pills in the other. My hand shook as I put the pills in my mouth. So cold. I downed them without asking what they were.

"Hey, Paige ..." His cheerfulness dissolved in an instant. "We've got to get you warm."

He pulled my rain jacket off. I wondered how he knew my name. He had probably spied on my rental agreement at the moped rental place. I was so tired I didn't even care. He pulled off my wellies and wet socks, throwing everything aside, and guided me out of the chair.

I was going to tell him wet clothes shouldn't be on wood floors, but I couldn't really form the words of such a long thought. I was unsteady on my feet. Within a moment, he had taken most of my weight onto him and half carried me up the stairs. He walked me into my aunt's bathroom like he owned the place. When he started to peel off my wet clothes, I put my foot down. "No."

"This time of year, you can't be too careful about hypothermia." He sat me on the edge of the tub.

"Go away." I shook with cold. It was all I could get out of my mouth. He pulled the wool sweater over my head, being careful to widen the neck so as to not touch the back of my head.

"Hey," he said softly. "It's okay. I've seen it all before. I'm on the emergency response crew."

"You haven't seen *me* before." Some part of my brain knew I wasn't making the most sense. "Stop."

"Please, we've got to get you warm. Hypothermia is a real thing."

"Please," I repeated. I just wanted to go to sleep on the floor and curl up in some towels. Maybe then I would wake up and this would all have been a bad dream. I was starting to feel oddly warm.

"Look, I'll stand on the other side of the door as long as you can get yourself out of those wet clothes and into a warm shower." He reached beyond us and turned on the shower faucet.

"Deal." I pushed his hands away and stood unsteadily.

"Can I trust that you'll call out if you need help? I'll be right outside."

The bathroom started to fill with warm clouds of mist. He adjusted the temperature of the water.

"Okay." One-word sentences were all I could manage right now. I put my hand out and steadied myself against the wall.

He looked concerned and like he didn't trust me. And I didn't even know if he could. I might have been making promises my body couldn't keep.

"I'm good. Go." I waved my hand half-heartedly at him.

He twitched his finger at me like I was a wayward child. "If I hear anything concerning, I'm coming right in. Don't lock the door, or I'll break it down."

Thinking about him breaking down the door seemed incredibly and oddly silly. I giggled despite everything. That seemed to reassure him, even though it made me *more* concerned. After all, nothing was funny. Was hilarity a sign of hypothermia?

He closed the door behind him. "Get into the shower, Paige," he yelled through the wood between us.

I did what he told me, and got in, without even stripping off my clothes. I really wasn't thinking straight. But the warm water felt amazing. I stood in the stream, both hands on the tile wall, feeling the first good sensation of the night. Well, second. His arms around me outside in the storm had felt so safe. And more than safe. Electrifying. Warmth started in my nether region, and ran through my whole body. I wondered what his touch would feel like without my clothes on ...

"Paige?" He said my name so softly it was like he was in the room with me, and I imagined his hands all over my body. Lighting my skin up.

"Mm-hmmm?"

"Gotta give me more, or I'm coming back in."

For a split second, I imagined letting him break back in, take me in his arms, caress every inch of my skin with his warm, callused hands. Flowing over me like the water. All over me. Every place, and then his fingers inside of me. I almost gasped.

"Paige!"

The daydream floated away with his command. "I'm fine! I'm in the shower! Feeling better …" So much better.

"Okay. Good."

I grabbed the soap in my hand. And then realized how ridiculous that was—I was still completely dressed. I struggled to pull my drenched shirt over my head.

"I'm good! I've got this. You can go. I'll come down when I'm done for proof of life." I was feeling much better, and able to think —and speak—in sentences again.

"All right. I'll be right downstairs. Yell if you need me." Clearly, he thought I was feeling better enough to leave me be.

I poked my head out of the shower to hear his creaky steps walk away back downstairs. I peeled off my bra and then got to work on my pants. When I got to my underwear, I couldn't help but imagine his hands pulling them off me. I leaned against the wall. Enjoying the thought. I couldn't deny that my body responded to him. Fantasy was totally fine. It wasn't like I was really going to start something up with the island guy I just met. I let my hands roam and feel good all over my body.

He had just saved me—if he hadn't come upon me, I didn't know what would have happened. I wanted to think I could have figured it out, made it back to the house myself, but it was hard to imagine. What wasn't hard to imagine was him in the shower with me. Touching me. Kissing my mouth, pressing his body against mine …

Wait. How *did* he find me? And how did he know my name? Coming by to check on my aunt's house—could I believe that explanation? Was he stalking me? The electricity coursing through my body from my fantasy turned to hot anger. I quickly washed my hair before turning off the water and stomping out of the shower. I wrapped my aunt's thick towel around me and I ran into the bedroom. Surveyed the strewn clothes on the floor and grabbed the first items in my reach. Yoga pants and a sweatshirt. I heard pounding from downstairs. What was he doing?

In spite of myself, or maybe because of the part of myself that had been totally into the fantasy of him in the shower, I stopped to brush my hair before heading back downstairs. No need to look like a crazy person.

I found him picking up twigs and debris beneath the now boarded-up, tree-less window. How long had I been in the shower?

"Good job," he said as if taking a shower was a monumental feat. He pounded in one more nail before grabbing a mug, filling it with coffee, and bringing it to me. "Sugar? Milk?" he asked.

I shook my head. I didn't want sugar and didn't have any milk. He put the mug in my hands and then went back to get another black cup of coffee and perched on a stool like we were just coffee-buddies hanging out. Outside it looked less dark. I checked my smartwatch, which was somehow still working after getting soaked in the storm and in the shower. Four-thirty-five. The coffee smelled yummy and I held the warm mug in both hands. Why couldn't I stay mad at this guy?

Because he keeps doing nice things and saved your life. Duh, Paige.
"How did you find me out there?" I sat on a stool two down from his.

"I could see your flashlight bobbing from the road. And then I didn't see it anymore. I went from thinking that someone was breaking into the house to scared that someone might have fallen into the bog." He shook his head. "You can't imagine the trouble mainlanders get here, not respecting the ocean or nature. Storms are unpredictable here."

"I'm not stupid. I wouldn't go out in the storm without a good reason!"

"Well, why didn't you call emergency services for help? That branch was heavy."

Clearly not too heavy for him. I ran my eyes down the bulky muscles showing through his tight thermal shirt. I thought about those arms around me again. "My cell died. And I thought I could do it on my own." *Stop thinking sexy thoughts about the stranger in your aunt's kitchen, Paige!*

"And the electricity was out, so you couldn't use the house phone." He nodded. I didn't correct him to say it hadn't even thought of a house phone. He gulped down some coffee.

I took a sip. It was yummy. Warmed my insides. Almost as much as my fantasy ... *STOP PAIGE.*

My eyes roamed over his body in spite of myself. "How are you dry? I got soaked even underneath my aunt's heavy-duty rain jacket." I closed my eyes so I didn't think any more embarrassing thoughts about his muscles and arms but closing my eyes didn't actually help.

"I had rain pants and a couple of waterproof layers on. Getting wet when it's this cold out can be dangerous. As you now know from experience." He grinned a lop-sided grin at me.

"Thank you for boarding up the window. For helping me. Thank you."

He shrugged. Like it was no big deal at all. Like rescuing mainlanders hitting their heads on rocks in a storm was just a normal Saturday. His eyes took in my aunt's cheery kitchen and then clouded like the storm. And that was the first time I thought about all the people on the island who might have been friends with my aunt. I looked closer at his deep eyes and knew I was seeing sorrow.

"You seem to know your way around my aunt's house." He hadn't just known where things were downstairs, he knew exactly where the bathroom was off my aunt's room. Everyone I knew in Boston had been in the bathroom off of my bedroom, but in a house this size, there would be no need. Unless you were really close.

"We were friends, your aunt and I. Well, more than friends, really. She was ... a part of the family."

Memories of my aunt flooded back. "For me too." Which was

pretty stupid to say, since she literally was my family. But he just smiled.

"She was really special. One of a kind." His voice sounded wistful. I wondered what he was thinking about. I shouldn't be surprised he knew her—everyone probably knew everyone else living on an island this small. He looked out at the first rays of sun coming over the bog. The rain was slowing, like its job was done. His next words were so quiet I almost missed them. "Spent a lot of time here."

Something buzzed and he pulled out his phone. I wondered where I had abandoned my phone in the darkness of the night. Hopefully not outside. Please, nighttime gods, let me have had the sense to have left it inside while I was out in the rain.

"Sorry to leave you with this mess," he waved his hands over the debris-filled, water-logged, eat-in nook. "You'll want to clean up the water as fast as you can today so your aunt's stuff doesn't get ruined. I have a call about a downed tree blocking a road on the other side of the island. Everyone else on the rescue crew is busy dealing with other storm issues. I'll stop by later to see if you need anything else."

"Don't worry about it. I'll get a handle on this, and then probably just take a nap." I was pretty certain I would see Jesse in my dreams. I tried to shake the image out of my head. Ow. I hoped he didn't notice my wince.

"All right." He donned all his rain gear and then stood in the middle of the kitchen, running his hand through his hair. "Let me look at your head one last time."

"I'm fine, really."

But he wouldn't take no for an answer. He ran his fingers up my scalp and I closed my eyes. Glad he was behind me and he couldn't see my expression. What was wrong with me? I didn't normally have this response to guys. Well, maybe that wasn't quite true. I did start my last relationship with a one-night stand. Thank goodness Matt was a great guy. Especially after the mess of things with Frank. Thinking of Frank scared all the sexy out of the situation.

He parted my hair and didn't say anything for a moment. "I think it's okay. Just a bump, and it's no longer bleeding. Definitely doesn't need stitches. But if you get a bad headache, head over to the hospital, please. You know the way?"

That was a surprise; I hadn't realized it had ever been bleeding. "I do. It's probably the one place I know on the island." I couldn't find my way to my aunt's house without directions, but I did know how to get to her hospital. There were signs for it all over the place.

He texted something into his phone. Clearly, his mind was already on his next storm adventure. He got up and wandered toward the front door.

"Thanks again!" I walked him out.

"No worries." He distractedly waved his hand in my direction before taking the steps two at a time and jogging to his truck. The rain was light now. I closed the door quickly behind him.

All I wanted was to sink into bed, but he was right. If I left water pooling on the table and floors, there would be damage.

I got to it right away. It took a few hours of clean-up, partly because I had to keep looking for buckets, mops, and cleaning supplies. By the time I threw the many towels I used on the mess in the washing machine, I could hardly see straight. I pulled off my clothes, pulled on new dry pajamas, and fell into my aunt's bed, not even bothering to close the blinds to block out the bright sun. Happy the storm was over, and happy to have escaped relatively unscathed. Boxing up my aunt's stuff would have to wait until later, which would throw my schedule behind at least a day. I closed my eyes and hoped for dreamless sleep. I turned into the soft pillow and pulled the warm blankets over me.

4

Aunt Del's bed was so comfortable I didn't want to get up. The room was bathed in the bright light of midday. I consulted my Magic Eight Ball keychain.

"Should I go to town now and order a new window?"

It took a moment for the triangle to drift up to the top of the ball so I could read it through the tiny window.

IT IS CERTAIN.

Ugh. But the Eight Ball was right. The quicker I ordered the window, the faster I could get this all sewn up. Get back to real life.

I shuffled out of bed and tried to re-orient myself. Downed some Tylenol to help combat the lingering headache. I made a list of all the things I had to do and half of the things were because of the storm damage. If I was going to get it all done, this week, I'd have to get a move on. My hair stuck up in all directions and bent in weird ways since I fell asleep while it was still wet. I jumped back into the shower to wet it again. It was like a redo to the start of the day. Too bad it was already mid-day.

I ran the brush through my hair but skipped all the normal face/hair morning rituals. I was on vacation. No need to primp.

I sorted the clothes strewn on the floor into two piles—wet and nearly dry. I took the wet clothes down to the washing machine and threw in a small load.

As I started the coffee machine, I imagined Jesse in the kitchen. In fact, everywhere I went in the house, I saw him. Which was kinda nice, because it replaced the feeling of emptiness in the house without my aunt. Maybe he'd come back and check on me. I wandered downstairs, imagining that scenario.

My cell phone was hiding inside the front closet. I had been like a squirrel the night before—leaving the phone in exchange for the flashlight and candles. I plugged it in next to the coffee pot in the kitchen. I could find my way back to town, so I wouldn't really need it for anything today. Although, I would miss any work calls I got, which was probably for the best.

With my coffee in a metal to-go-cup, and Aunt Del's wellies on my feet, I surveyed the damage outside. The bog was beautiful in daylight. Birds chirped, insects buzzed, along with other animal noises I couldn't identify. The branch that Jessie had pulled from the window was huge. I wandered around until I found the rock that I probably had hit my head on. There were lots of rocks underneath the grass, so anywhere I would have slipped, I would have most likely hit something hard.

Looking back up at my aunt's beautiful Victorian with weathered shingles, the boarded-up window looked like a black eye on the otherwise pristine house. Time to get that fixed.

I ditched my coffee mug on the front porch since I couldn't figure out how to safely ride with a cup in my hand, hopped on the moped and headed slowly into town, realizing that I was starving. Had I had more than coffee in the last eighteen hours?

I hadn't paid much attention to the strip of businesses just off the ferry dock in the rain yesterday. There were some upscale tourist shops, a cafe, and a general store. The moped shack was set apart, at the end.

The Oceanside Cafe looked perfect. My stomach growled unhappily. I parked the moped and walked in. It was empty of customers. I checked my watch and realized it was already three p.m. I had slept most of the day!

"Hello dear, be right with you." A kind-looking man was slowly wiping a table down in the corner. "Sit anywhere."

I sat at a table overlooking the street, and then beyond, the beach and water. I could see the ferry dock as well. Everything looked washed and new in the post-storm sunshine. The man brought over a paper menu/placemat with a map of the island on the back. "Are you here for the day?"

"A little longer than that. I'm putting my aunt's house in order. What's your favorite on the menu?" I always asked that. I figured when in Rome, eat like the locals.

"Everyone loves the pancakes. I do too, but my wife wants me to eat healthy, so I save them for special occasions. We also have lunch items if you prefer. But we're known for the pancakes."

"I love a place that has breakfast all day. Pancakes it is. And coffee too. With milk."

He grabbed a syrup caddy from the next table over and placed it on my table. "Your aunt?"

"Delilah Givens." I knew I should say more, but her name brought a lump to my throat. I guess I hadn't said it aloud much since she died.

He nodded, looking sad himself. Then he said over his shoulder, "Penny, come meet Del's niece."

A smart-dressed older woman came out from the kitchen, wiping her hands on the half-apron tied around her waist. "Del's niece? Oh, honey, we're so sorry for your loss. I'm Penny, this is my husband, Walter, who never remembers to introduce himself."

"Paige." I put out my hand and Penny grabbed it, pulled me out of the chair, and into a bear hug. The best momma-bear hug ever. I couldn't help myself; tears ran down my cheeks. When she let me go, I mumbled an apology for being emotional and wiped my cheeks with the tiny diner napkins from the steel napkin holder.

"Don't ever apologize for feeling things. If I could get Walter to feel more, our relationship would be perfect." She swatted at him. Clearly trying to lighten the mood and make me feel better. I felt a burst of gratefulness for her.

"What are you talking about? Our relationship is perfect. Well, you're perfect." Walter grabbed Penny, did a waltz step, and dipped her. He kissed her softly on the lips before letting her go.

"Your pancakes will be up shortly—when the cafe is this empty, I can hear a pin drop. I heard you order them." She pulled Walter back toward the kitchen. "Let's give Paige some space."

I flipped over the paper placemat menu and to my delight, there was a cartoon map of the island with businesses and tourist attractions listed.

Before long, Walter came back out carrying a giant stack of flapjacks. He didn't linger but left to let me dive right in.

The pancakes were light and fluffy and perfect. I wolfed them down, hoping that Penny and Walter and whoever was at the grill in the kitchen weren't watching my terrible eating etiquette. Studying the map of the island, I decided the general store looked like the best place to inquire about ordering a new bay window.

The bell rang over the diner and a woman my age wearing shorts with construction boots strode in. She wasn't even to the counter before Penny called out from the back, "Bells, we're just putting your order together now. We wanted the coffee to be hot."

The girl had her hair in one braid down her back. She surveyed my clean plate and smiled.

"The pancakes are the best, aren't they?"

I nodded. "The best."

She leaned casually against the counter. "You here for a vacation?"

"Kind-of." I oddly wasn't bothered that everyone wanted to know my story. I was feeling happy and sleepy after the pancakes. I sipped the coffee, hoping the caffeine would sink in at some point.

"I know, right? I came here after college to help my grandparents and then stayed. It's so beautiful. If there were only more cute guys, it would be perfect."

Maybe the lack of sleep made me blurt out, "I don't know, the guy I met yesterday seemed pretty cute."

Penny appeared out of nowhere. "Oh, tell me, who'd you meet?" She put a drink carrier full of coffee cups on the counter in front of the girl, along with a brown bag.

Somehow, this didn't seem like gossiping. After all, I had no info about this guy who seemed to show up wherever I was. I suddenly wanted as much info about him as I could get. "Jesse?"

"Oh, swoon. Yeah, he's something. Not my type, though, because we work together—that would just be too awkward. He's so nice, though. I'm Bells, short for Isabel."

I stood and shook her hand. "Paige. I'm Doctor Delilah Givens' niece. Nice to meet you."

"Oh, my goodness. I'm so sorry. And me going on about cute island guys! Anyone who is family to Del is family to, well, everyone. We take care of our own. If there's anything I can do just let me know." Bells looked like she wanted to hug me or cry, or both. Instead, she paced the small diner. "Most nights off I'm at Magnolia's. The bar off of Water Street. Not because I drink a lot, but because my friends own it. And they have good food." She grabbed her to-go order.

Over her shoulder on the way out the door, she said, "Penny, you can only come if you don't misbehave this time."

That cracked me up. Thinking about what Penny, clearly in her sixties, could do to misbehave. Penny didn't elaborate but smiled widely. "Did you weather the storm okay, Paige?"

"A tree branch fell into my aunt's window." I skipped the part where I was rescued by Jessie. "Where do I go to replace it?"

"Oh, if I had known—Bells can help you with that. She works at the general store. She'll send someone out to measure and then they'll order it from the mainland. Might take a week or so to come in, much more if it's a custom order, and Jesse would help install it." Her smile grew even larger.

Clearly, she was shipping Jesse and me in her head. Hell, I was shipping Jesse and me in my head, and it had to stop. Even though he didn't seem anything like Frank, Frank didn't seem anything like Frank when I first met him. He had seemed like a normal guy. The controlling came later.

Plus, I was only here for a few days.

She took my plate and pointed to the right. "Island General is a couple of doors down. Your pancakes are on the house. Go get your window ordered."

"I can pay—please."

"You're Del's niece." She smiled sadly at me. "Just come back to eat here again, and we'll call it even."

"Okay." *See Jesse, I can accept help when offered by a sensible individual.* Why was I talking to him in my thoughts? I shook it off, gathered myself, thanked Penny again, and went in search of the general store.

★★★

Island General was aptly named. It sold a little of everything. The front of the store was clearly geared toward tourists; beach umbrellas, sun hats, and even bathing suits lined the front aisles. The back looked more like a hardware store. But as I looked around, I found that there was one of everything that anyone could possibly need. One type of toaster, one type of rat trap, one type of fireworks.

I bypassed the initial counter and cash register, nodding to the man behind the counter, and headed to the construction section. Bells sat back there, perched on another counter, sipping a coffee and munching on a poppyseed muffin.

"Hey, Paige. Want a muffin?" She held the brown bag out to me. This island certainly didn't mind offering things to strangers for free.

"I'm good, thanks." I rubbed my stomach. "I may not even need dinner—those pancakes were so filling."

"If Penny had her way, everyone on the island would be 400 pounds. Except for Walter, of course—he's had some health scares. But those pancakes are like love to her. And she loves everyone here. How can I help you?"

"I need to order a bay window. The storm sent a branch through my aunt's window."

Bells nodded. "I'll just come out and measure it this afternoon and we'll get it ordered." She picked up a notebook that looked like it had been war-torn. She ran her finger down a page with writing scrawled halfway down it. She stopped at the last entry. "Weird."

"What?" I tried to read the scribbled words upside-down but couldn't make them out.

"Jesse already ordered you one."

"Really?" Was there nothing he wouldn't meddle in?

"Yup." She hopped off the counter and stood beside me, turning the book so I could read it. "See here?" Her finger tapped at the words: Bay Storm Window 81 x 50 inches. "That's Jesse's handwriting."

"My ears are burning. What about me?" Jesse sauntered up in a black cotton tee and jeans.

Free pancakes were one thing, but this guy overstepping his bounds by taking matters into his own hands to fix my aunt's house? Such a Frank move. Controlling and meant for me to be in his debt? I didn't think so.

I turned away from Jesse and pretended that it was just Bells and me in the back of the store. "Let's cancel that order. Please do come out and measure today."

Bells handed Jessie a muffin.

"No need. Measuring's done. Ordering's done. Luckily it's a standard size window, and in stock. I got the order into OC on the mainland in time for this Friday's delivery. If you cancel the order, it'll take an extra week—won't be here until a week from Friday." He took a bite from his muffin.

I fumed.

After he swallowed, he said, "But do what you want."

"Coffee, Jesse?" Bells had a crazy grin on her face. Was everyone on this island shipping Jesse and me?

"Nope, Paige was kind enough to give me coffee in the middle of the night. I'm heading out to get some shut-eye. I just came to let you know that I dropped the order to the Baskins already."

"What is your deal?" I turned to him.

"I'd give you privacy, but this is too much fun. Plus, Paige, I've got your back." Bells was clearly enjoying all this.

"As you should, although, Bells, does our years of friendship mean nothing to you?" Jesse seemed to be enjoying this as well.

Which made me even more infuriated. "Look, I appreciate your help last night, but you can stop now. Stop stalking me, stop trying to anticipate my needs. I can handle my own life, thank you. Bells, let me know when you want to get together for a girls' night." After all, she did say she had my back. I turned quickly, intending to storm out, but instead tripped over a stack of paint cans, narrowly catching my balance on a nearby shelf. Dammit. So much for looking like I had everything under control.

"Hey," he grabbed my arm to steady me. "Is your head okay? Maybe we should take you in to check for a concussion."

"I don't have a concussion; I'm just really tired. It makes me clumsy." For some reason, I felt like bursting into tears. And then I did.

Jesse's hand on my arm was replaced by a smaller one, and Bells put her other arm around my back. "Jesse, I got this, okay?" Her voice was low, sweet, and commanding all at the same time. She steered me into a back room.

Directing me to a comfy office chair, she pulled out a folding chair and sat next to me, pulling me into her shoulder.

"I'm so sorry. I don't know what ..." I buried myself in her shirt and couldn't believe I was breaking down so publicly.

"Shhhhh. Let it out. You lost your aunt. Anyone would be sad." She grabbed a box of tissues and put it in my hands.

"My aunt's house ... without her. I didn't sleep at all last night and I hit my head. And Jesse. He was so nice. But they all start that way. My nice ex is far away and my controlling ex is still trying to get back into my life." I was ugly-crying in front of a stranger. And I couldn't stop. "I'm sorry!"

"That's a lot." She pulled me closer to her. "I broke up with someone recently too. Totally my fault. Or his. I don't know. Life is ... life, you know. I miss your aunt too. She was something. Made everyone feel so special."

"She did." I pulled my head back and wiped the tears from my face. "She really did."

"You know, there was one time when she ordered tiki torches for a party she threw with Sylvi but I guess she ordered them in between patients she was taking care of and wasn't paying attention. She ordered 100 instead of ten and ended up giving everyone who came to the party tiki torches as favors. Everyone in town pretty much ended up with a tiki torch of their own, whether they wanted one or not!"

I started laughing. "I can totally picture her doing that." Bells giggled too. Soon we were cracking up.

"I should go." I stood and grabbed a tissue from the box and blew my nose.

"Do you feel like you can get home okay? I can take you to the hospital if you think it's your head. Better to get medical care now than have it be a bigger thing later." Bells stood too and rubbed my arm.

"I'm really okay. I only got a few hours of sleep, and think I just need to go take a nap or something." I ignored the fact that I was swaying on my feet.

"Rest up. I'll come over Tuesday to help pack up your aunt's stuff. That's too much to tackle alone." Bells held my arms and I felt stronger, and less alone.

"You don't have to ..."

"I insist. Del was a rockstar on this island. Any relative of hers is automatic family to those who knew her. Plus, we women have to stick together. Double plus, I have so many more stories about your aunt. Triple plus, I'd love to hear yours."

I was too tired and relieved to insist I could do it all on my own. I could suddenly see why Aunt Del decided to move to this island.

"You know Jesse is waiting outside to see if you're okay. He went through his own thing last year losing someone close. It's hard for him to see anyone in pain. Give him a break, okay? He's a good guy." She let go of my arms and rubbed my back.

I nodded. I was too tired to do anything else.

Bells opened the office door. "Hey Jesse, we're coming out. Your girl needs some space and a nap."

I touched my puffy face. I must look awful. I just wanted to be back at my aunt's house and away from prying island eyes. Actually, I wanted to be transported back to the safety of my apartment in Boston. I never cried in front of people, especially not strangers. But there wasn't anything I could do about it now, except get on my moped as quickly as possible.

"Got it. But ..." Jesse crossed his arms across his chest. I was sure he was going to insist on driving me to the hospital. Bells sternly shook her head. Her face looked scary, suddenly. I giggled. Wow. My emotions were all over the place. And too close to the surface. And I was starting to realize how good it was to have Bells in my corner.

I navigated through the cluttered aisles in the store, this time without knocking anything over, and out into the blinding sunlight.

★★★

I didn't even remember driving home—suddenly I was parking the moped in the sandy driveway in front of Aunt Del's. But I knew if I went back to bed, my days and nights would be all screwed up. No matter how painful it would be, I had to keep myself awake. I was too tired—and emotional—to attack my aunt's things. I decided the only way to keep myself up was to be out in the sunlight.

I found the deck furniture in the garage and dragged a loveseat, two chairs, and a table to the side of the wrap-around porch. I set them up on the back deck, imagining what the storm would have done with these if they had been out last night. Projectiles flying at the house for sure. I made a mental note to put the furniture away when I was done.

I went inside long enough to brew more coffee and grab my laptop. Then I settled into the loveseat outside and answered some work emails, enjoying the view into the now-friendly-looking bog. Five p.m. If I could just stay awake another couple of hours, I wouldn't screw up my days and nights that bad.

The sun was warm and comfortable and the distant sound of waves crashing somewhere nearby lulled me into a dreamlike state. I was exhausted to my core after my crying jag.

But somehow, I also felt cleaned out, as if I had needed to storm a little bit to feel some peace. I pulled my feet onto the loveseat and put the laptop on the table. I closed my eyes, just for a second. Of course, Jesse was the one I saw behind my eyelids.

I reassured myself. Fantasies are perfectly fine.

If I asked the Eight Ball app, I was sure it would tell me: WITHOUT A DOUBT.

5

"You really shouldn't sleep outside."
I opened my eyes, into a bright floodlight which blinded me. Beyond the white light, darkness hid the frogs and grasshoppers that chirped in the bog and an owl hooted in the distance. Had I dreamt his voice?

"It's not safe."

I shrieked. Jumped up. Jesse was standing on the porch, looking at me.

"Oh. My. God. Stalk much? What is *wrong* with you?"

Jessie held up his hands defensively. "I'm sorry. I just wanted to make sure the board held. It wasn't my best work, in the middle of a storm at night. I thought I'd just sneak back, secure it a bit more, and you wouldn't even know I was here. But here you are, sleeping OUTSIDE."

"And that makes it better? That you were going to sneak into my backyard without me knowing? Isn't that the definition of stalking? Couldn't you plan on ringing the doorbell, during the light of day?"

"You're totally right." He ran his hand through his hair, which was totally cute, even though I was pissed at him. Fantasy Me wanted to run my hands through his hair and see what it felt like.

Clearly, I was my own worst enemy when it came to shutting down this crush.

"I was up all night, then worked a half-day and went home and fell asleep. When I woke up, I just wanted to check on you. I know it's stupid, but I just worried ..." His voice trailed off.

Maybe he was sincere. Maybe I didn't need to be so hard on him. Bells' words about him losing someone close reminded me that you just never know what's going on with someone beneath the surface. I smiled up at him. "Thanks for thinking of me." Still groggy, Fantasy Me was still thinking of running my hands through his hair, then down his back to his butt which I bet was tight ... *oh, my god, give it a break, Paige!*

"I really am sorry. I'll give you some space, I promise. After I check the plank."

In spite of myself, (or my fantasy self), I watched the floodlights accentuate every inch of him as he drilled a couple of screws into the board over the window. I swore I could see his muscles flex beneath the thin cotton shirt. and then he walked past me on the deck without saying anything. The floodlight illuminated his ass ...

"Jesse!"

He turned.

"Thank you."

He smiled a half-smile and shoved his hands in his pocket as he turned the corner of the deck. His truck revved up in the distance and I listened until it faded off in the distance.

I gathered up my things and went inside. Had a quick dinner of a peanut butter and jelly sandwich, checked my phone, which was all charged up and actually working, and headed upstairs to go back to sleep.

Sleep wouldn't come—of course not—I had accidentally slept most of the day. The creaks and groans of the house reminded me of how alone I was. It was one thing being alone in the daylight, but being wide awake and by myself for hours during the night felt totally lonely. Was I going to be up all night?

I might as well get some work done packing up my aunt's things. I went downstairs and surveyed the library. I'd need piles to keep things straight.

I wrote out paper labels, one marked 'keep,' the other 'charity.'

Where to start? Categorizing Aunt Del's life seemed so ... final. Who was I to decide what was important and what wasn't?

I just sat there staring at my aunt's neat and orderly life. At ten p.m., I decided to give up. Maybe nighttime wasn't the best time to try to do such a hard thing. I didn't feel like working on marketing work either.

I smoothed out the table-setting map I had tucked in my pocket from the diner. There was one bar mentioned. Should I go blow off some steam, Magic Eight Ball? I shook the tiny keychain and squinted to read the result. AS I SEE IT, YES. So, it was unanimous.

I threw on jeans and a silk t-shirt and sweater and hopped on the moped. It felt good starting to find my way around.

Magnolia's was quiet for a Saturday night. Probably because it wasn't yet tourist season. An old-fashioned jukebox sat in the corner pounding out tunes. A row of pool tables lined the wall on the right, and a smattering of tables took up the rest of the room. Next to a small stage, the bar itself was in the back center of the room. I made a beeline for it. I wasn't going to drink anything harder than soda—I just had a hankering for human contact. The female bartender wore a black t and wiped the counter in front of me as I sat down.

"What would you like?"

"Ginger ale, please."

Her eyebrows raised but she didn't say a thing. Before I knew it, a tall glass filled with ice and clear soda sat in front of me.

"You here on vacation?" She was a good bartender; I could already tell. She had that perfect combination of interest and aloofness that told me that I could tell her my secrets and she cared enough to listen, but not enough to pass along. With a good bartender around, who needed a therapist?

"Actually, no." If I couldn't open up to a bartender I was never going to see again, who could I open up to? "I'm boxing up all the stuff in my aunt's house. Keeping the important things for the family; giving the rest to charity." Correction: that was what I wasn't doing right now.

"I'm sorry. That must be tough."

"Tough is right. I've been on the island for almost thirty-six hours and haven't even gotten started. I got waylaid by last night's storm. And then slept all day. So, when I tried to attack it tonight, it just seemed ... hard. How do I choose what was important to my aunt? What to keep? What to pass along?"

"Sounds like you need a little help." A good therapist, bartender, and smart too.

"You're right. And today someone offered to help me." I had forgotten that until right now. "Thanks for the advice. I'm Paige, by the way."

"Margo. Nice to meet you."

"Come here often?" Jesse sat on the tall bar stool beside me. My pulse picked up.

"Hey, Jesse. Great to see you tonight." Margo smiled warmly and busied herself by wiping down the already spotless bar top.

"Seriously? And you say you're *not* stalking me?" I shook my head. But, in the light of a friendly, happy, buzzing bar, his actions over the past couple of days felt sweet. After all, everyone I met seemed to think highly of him. Penny, Bells, and now Margo.

Margo grinned, probably because my tone sounded kind and not at all harsh. "What can I get you, Jesse?"

"Rum and Coke. A little caffeine, a little fun." He turned to me. "I think it's official—my days and nights are reversed. How about you?" His face was open and interested.

Suddenly I wanted to run my hands ALL over his body. *Reign it in, Paige.* "Too tired to work; too awake to sleep."

Margo handed him his drink, and he held it up. "To Mother Nature and all she throws our way."

When I didn't raise my glass to his, he clinked mine where it sat. I wasn't sure where I stood with Mother Nature, but I certainly wasn't going to tempt her to throw anything more at me.

After taking a swig, Jesse asked, "Margo, are you closing the bar tonight, or are you off soon so you can have a drink with us?"

"As soon as Rachel gets here, we'd be happy to join you for one drink." She buffed the counter. "I'm off an hour before closing tonight. She's stopping by to bike home with me."

"Great!" He turned to me. "Shall we grab a table? Do you want to play pool?"

It was nice how quickly I had gone from tourist to local on the island. And how quickly Jesse had pulled me into his inner circle.

My body knew exactly how far away he sat and how little it would take to bridge the gap. Why was my mind working so hard to resist? An island fling might just be what would set me right. "Margo, I'll take a Dark and Stormy, if you don't mind."

"Nice." Jesse clinked my glass again.

"Dark rum?" Margo asked.

"Of course!" I nodded to Jesse. "Let's find a table."

Drinks in hand, Jesse steered me to a vacant table on the edge of the pool tables. I settled in with my drink, and Jesse started pointing out the people in the bar and telling stories about them. He had a story for everyone. "And that's Toph and John. Always splitting up and getting back together. Everyone thinks they will end up together, except them."

"Do you know everyone?" I had always thought that small-town life, and in this case, small island life, would be claustrophobic, but right now it seemed like those towns in movies where everyone helped everyone else. Sort-of magical. And funny. I laughed more than I had in months, hearing about a kid walking off a dock, library book in hand, and a tourist forgetting to untie a dingy before motoring away from a pier.

"Not nearly everyone. The island is larger than it seems. And outside my circle of friends, I keep to myself unless somebody needs something, you know?"

That made me laugh so hard I almost fell off my stool. As if he had kept to himself where I was concerned. I had seen him how many times in the past twenty plus hours?

He ran his hand through his hair, which I was now finding adorable. And sexy. "I know a good thing when I see one. And you are a very good thing."

Being called a good *thing* didn't normally sound so great, but out of Jesse's mouth, it sounded amazing.

"I know I came on strong—am still coming on strong, really. Something happened last year that made me realize how fragile life can be. Quick. Unexpected. I mean, it's impossible to live on an island and not realize that, really. But this past year ..."

I put my hand over his and didn't say anything. Just felt the connection between us. Losing my aunt had made me feel the same way. I hadn't seen Aunt Del all the time, but she was someone who had always been there. Someone who I always thought *would* be there. An anchor of sorts for my life.

Life was short and suddenly all I wanted was Jesse in it. The rum was working its magic and I was feeling like letting all my imaginings about this man come true.

I gazed at Jesse, and he looked deep into my eyes. I had the strongest urge to close the distance between us and taste his lips. I leaned in ever so slightly. He put his hand on my thigh.

My phone buzzed. I leaned away from him to see who was calling. "My mom. I should take this." I pushed my chair back to get up.

"Stay put. I'll get us a few more drinks."

"Jesse?"

He turned to me.

"Don't think you were saved by the bell—I'm totally kissing you tonight."

He moved so quickly it sent chills down my spine. He closed the distance between us, pulled me from the chair, held my face between his hands, and his lips were on mine for the briefest moment. I could taste cold rum and coke and *him*. I closed my eyes. My whole body responded, but he was suddenly gone—walking to the bar—and grinning widely back at me.

Oh my god, was he sexy.

I clicked the answer button on my phone. "Hey, Mom." I put the phone to my ear and sat back down. My mom's voice rattled happily over the miles and ocean between us.

Distractedly, and watching Jesse's every move, I filled in my side of the conversation. "Yes, I'm here ... No, I haven't really started boxing things up yet ... It's a little sad, but I've met people here who are going to help ... Yes, I still think I want to sell. I just don't know what I would do with island property ... Just a week." I watched Jessie chatting with Margo "... Or so..."

My mom shrieked into the phone and yelled about how she was burning cookies. She hung up without even saying goodbye.

Jesse sat back down and waved Bells over. She grinned as she pulled up a chair. I really liked her. And I didn't think she'd mind if I stole a kiss or two from Jesse while she was with us. The night was looking up. Way up.

My phone buzzed again and I held it to my ear without looking at it. "Did you rescue the cookies?"

"Nope, no cookies." It wasn't my mom's voice; it was a deep male voice. My heart sank. "Frank."

"You thought if you blocked my calls, I couldn't reach you."

What an asshole. What a controlling asshole. I *had* blocked his number. I looked at my phone. A 617 number I didn't recognize. He was calling from someone else's phone. I didn't ever pick up unknown number calls—but I had been sure it had been my mom calling back to say she had either nuked the cookies or saved them.

"Don't call me again." I hung up. Matt told me to call him if Frank started to bother me again, and my finger hovered over his number on my phone. But Matt was all the way in Texas. And I didn't need my considerate ex to handle my crazy ex.

"Did your mom upset you?" Jesse narrowed his eyes, and looked at me like I was perhaps a little crazy. After all, he barely knew me and I barely knew anyone on this island. No matter that we all had my aunt in common.

"Nope, just an ex." I grabbed the drink he set down in front of me and took a long gulp. Trying desperately to get back into the mood I was in two minutes ago. Feeling connected to Jesse. Wanting to be connected to Jesse. "So, let me get this straight. When there's danger on the island, it's your job to run right toward it? Without looking?"

"Oh, that's more me, not Jesse." Bells sat down across from me.

"I carefully survey the situation and then run toward it. Bells is right. She's the one who leaps before she looks. Gets into all sorts of trouble."

They both laughed and I tried to join in, but that phone call from Frank had really unnerved me. He had robbed me of my delirious post-kiss haze, and brought me back into real life, which didn't seem so magical anymore.

"What kind of trouble?" I took another swig of my drink, hoping to get back into a carefree mood.

"There was this one time Mrs. Brewster's cat was stuck up a tree ..."

"Oh my god, you're going to tell it all wrong. Let me explain what happened." Bells hands waved around emphatically. "So, Bingo was up a tree and Mrs. Brewster was freaking out. I told her it was no problem; I'd get him down. So, I shimmied up, and the cat went higher. So, I went higher. The next thing I knew, we were out on this branch. Bingo, that asshole cat, walked over me and backed his way down the tree. He left me on this branch that couldn't really hold my weight." She took another sip and raised her glass. "Not that I'm heavy, mind you."

"Heavier than a cat." Jesse smiled at me. I awkwardly smiled back.

"For sure! So, the branch starts cracking and I know I'm not going to be able to climb off of it in time. So, I yell out ..."

"Timber! She yells timber. Like she's felling the tree. And then she jumps out of the tree and does this amazing somersault. Really. I wish I had gotten it on video."

"Well, I was sure I'd get hurt if I went down with the branch, so I catapulted off the limb. Only sprained my ankle; I was fine. Got a standing ovation from the rest of the team."

"To saving cats!"

"And people flat on their back out in a storm!" I raised my glass.

"Wait, what?" Bells put her drink down.

"Jesse didn't tell you? I figured I was the talk of the town."

Jesse reached out and covered my hand with his. "Of course, I didn't tell anyone about that. It's not my story to tell." Instantly our connection was back. His touch made me feel safe but also made my skin buzz. Everywhere.

"What happened?"

"Nothing as interesting as your story—I was pulling a tree branch out of my aunt's window and slipped and hit my head, and Jesse found me." I finished my drink.

"Paige, I had no idea! We definitely should have taken you to the hospital today. Are you really okay? That could have been really bad. It got cold last night."

I shrugged. "I'm totally fine." I shook my head a bunch of times. "See? Totally fine." And a little drunk, evidently. So much for hanging out, drinking soda, and people-watching. But I was starting to have fun again.

Bells wandered off to say hello to someone and I inched my chair closer to Jesse's. He stared intently into my eyes.

"I'm waiting for that kiss you promised to give me earlier."

"Didn't we already kiss?" I didn't feel so drunk that I would have imagined something like that.

"I kissed you. I'm waiting for you to kiss me. Since you did promise. And I'm not feeling all that patient."

"Oh, it's like that?"

"It's like that."

I put my arms around him and pulled him to me. I looked

devilishly at him until he was so close that I closed my eyes and sunk my lips to him. Instead of gently caressing his lips, I pressed hard and pushed my tongue into his mouth. He groaned a little and I murmured in response.

For a moment, there was no one else in the room. I lost track of time and space before my awareness returned. *I'm kissing a stranger in the middle of a bar.* I detangled myself from him and sighed. Ever since Frank and I had broken up, I had been sorta reckless with love. Well, last time it was a deliberate one-night stand. This certainly didn't feel like a one-night stand.

He leaned in to touch his forehead to mine. "I'm really glad I saved you in the storm last night. Totally worth it."

I swatted at him with my hand. "Do you get this kind of a response every time you help someone on the island?"

"If only. I'd take this in lieu of a salary!"

Bells came over, with Margo, and a girl and a guy I didn't know. "Hey, Jesse, Rachel's bike has a flat. Do you have stuff in your truck to fix that?"

"Sure. Rachel, Xavier, this is Paige. Paige, Rachel, Xavier." We shook hands.

Jessie excused himself and Rachel and Margo went out with him. Xavier didn't say a word to me but left our table and joined a group of men at a pool table on the other side of the room.

Bells had just sat started to tell me another story about a non-emergency rescue on the island—some mainlanders in a boat with engine trouble drifting into the cove—when Jesse returned.

"Hey, I don't have my patch kit here, so I'm going to drive Rachel and Margo home. He turned to me and put his hand on my arm. "You'll stay put?"

"We'll make sure she has fun while you're gone." In a stage whisper, Bells added, "We might have more fun, in fact!"

"Are you good to drive?" I put my arms around him, protectedly.

"I switched to just Coke after my first drink—anyone with one of the only trucks on the island has to be sober when the bar closes down—just for this sort of thing."

"Okay. Hurry back."

Bells and I continued to swap stories until it was close to closing. I went to pay my tab with a guy who introduced himself as Gus and who was now manning the bar.

"Jesse took care of that for you."

"Well, isn't he the chivalrous dude?"

"Yes, he is."

Bells nodded in agreement. "I'm going to head out. You good, Paige?"

I leaned into the bar. "I'll just finish this last drink and wait for Jesse."

She waved her fingers at me. "This doesn't count as girls' night —we'll have a super fun time when I don't have to work the next day. And I haven't forgotten. I'll be at your aunt's place bright and early on Tuesday. So, leave lots for me to do!"

And then it was just me, finishing up my drink.

My phone buzzed and I looked down at it. I had ten missed calls. Ten. Not one was from my mom with a cookie update. They were all from different 617 numbers. Frank. My happiness drained away and I worried. Since I had blocked his number, I had no idea if he was focusing on me and our breakup, or moving on. Calling ten times in less than an hour was excessive. Obsessive, really. I pulled on my sweater and decided to get some fresh air. How could I block all of these random Boston numbers?

Being outside didn't make me feel any less concerned about Frank's behavior. Was he okay? I shook my mini Magic Eight Ball. MY SOURCES SAY NO. Stupid ball. As concerned as I was, I didn't want to pick up his calls—that would just encourage him. And that wasn't good for either of us. We were solidly broken up. There was nothing I could do. Especially since I was on an island and he was back in Boston. I grabbed the moped and started walking down the street. I certainly wasn't in any shape to drive, but the movement made me feel more in control.

The moon hung low and ripe in the sky, giving me quite the guiding light. The way to my aunt's place was so much longer when not riding the moped.

Time seemed so slow that I didn't realize when I stopped walking forward. Maybe I could just rest on the moped for a minute.

It didn't even seem like a minute had passed before headlights flashed across me, and Jesse was suddenly beside me.

"Hey, sorry that took so long—they had a tree down across their driveway."

"And you moved it for them, that's sweet. You're sweet." And so not Frank.

"I've got that" He pulled a plank from his trunk bed, grabbed the moped, and I watched his bulging arms in the moonlight hoist it up the ramp and into the back of the truck. He walked me around to the cab, got me settled inside, and closed the door behind me. The truck was warm and cozy. The front seat was one bench seat so I slid across and I snuggled into him when he got in, because why not? "You're warm." And he was. So warm. I ran my hand over his t-shirt. Felt the taut muscles underneath.

"You're cute."

He put the car in gear and then pulled me even closer, keeping one arm around me. I closed my eyes. Before I knew it, the truck stopped and we were idling in front of my aunt's house.

"Thanks for the fun evening." His voice filled the warm cab.

I knew his words were supposed to make me get out of the car and walk into the house, but I was so comfortable. I could just sleep here. I didn't need to look into his eyes to know what they looked like. He had been looking at me all night at the bar like he wanted to protect me. Like I was the only thing in the world. I could get used to that.

"Mmm-hmmm." I nestled in closer.

"Paige?"

"Mmm-hmm?"

"I didn't realize how I wasn't really living my life until you showed up. Sometimes things happen and we just, you know, forget to pay attention. Just go through the motions. But when I saw you in the road ..."

"When you almost ran me down ..."

"When you walked recklessly in front of my truck, well, the world suddenly seemed alive with color. Like before it was grayish. And now it's vibrant."

"It's probably just because you almost killed me. But still. That's so nice to say."

"I'm not being nice." He gently pulled eased me up so he was looking into my eyes.

"What made your world lose color?" Those brown eyes got deeper in the moonlight.

"My sister died." He turned to look out the window. I didn't know what he was seeing, but it probably wasn't my aunt's house and wraparound porch in the moonlight. I waited to give him time. Maybe he'd tell me more. When the silence stretched on, I leaned back into him and held him. If I could make him feel just a tiny bit as safe as he made me feel, maybe he'd feel better.

And I felt like I could stay like this forever. Safe, warm, cherished. But eventually, we parted. He didn't say more, but got out of the cab, walked around to my door, and took my hand to help me down. And then his hand stayed in mine. Warm and strong.

He led me up the steps to the front door. I turned to face him, and as if half-asleep, or in a dream, I touched my lips gently to his. At that sensitive touch, electricity spun through me and I couldn't control myself. I pulled him in, pressing my body against his, and pushing my tongue insistently into his mouth.

He wrapped his arms around my body, one hand keeping pressure on my back, the other winding up to the base of my head. Holding me to him.

When the feeling of clothing over our bodies in the cool night became too much, I moaned.

He untangled himself. "Jeez, baby."

I put my hand on his chest, overwhelmed by my body's eagerness to explore him. "I'll see you tomorrow?"

"You better believe it." He shook his head and turned to walk back to the truck.

I made myself turn in walk into the house. I couldn't trust myself to be in his presence for another moment. I would rip his clothes off and take him right there, in the moonlight.

I was all the way up the stairs and into my aunt's room, flicking the light on as I went, before I heard the sound of his truck turning around on the gravel drive.

My dreams would be vivid tonight.

I shook the Magic Eight Ball to see if it agreed.

IT IS DECIDEDLY SO.

6

I woke in a puddle of sunlight, in my aunt's bed, thinking of the deep goodnight kiss we shared on the porch after we finally left his car. If I hadn't been so tired, I might have pulled him upstairs to bed.

For kicks, I turned to the Magic Eight Ball keychain on the bedside table and asked, "Should I have slept with Jesse last night?" The triangle drifted slowly to the top. ASK AGAIN LATER. Thanks for nothing, Eight Ball.

A quick look at my smartwatch let me know that it was dead. I hunted down its charger and plugged it into the wall. My phone only had a little charge left, but its cord was downstairs. I didn't know why there couldn't be one universal charger for everything in my life—so frustrating.

The clock on my phone said two pm. I had slept most of the day away again. Was it Tuesday yet? Had I missed Bells? Nope. Monday. Phew. I wanted to make some initial headway on the sorting-through process before Bells came by.

Coffee first. I stumbled downstairs and brewed a cup. While waiting, I started hunting around the kitchen. Opening up cabinets. Taking mental stock. My aunt had been relatively minimalist, but still, there was a lot of stuff. I found a narrow notepad, poured the coffee into a giant mug (again, I had forgotten to get any groceries so no almond milk for my coffee), and sat at the bar, looking over the bog.

I started with the most logical list: things I needed to buy in order to box up her stuff. Boxes. Sharpies. Tape. I planned on shipping any keepsakes to the members of the family who might want them—my mom, my other aunt, my brother, me. So, I'd need packing materials and bubble wrap.

The sun stretched into the kitchen and I wondered how warm it was outside. I grabbed my stuff and headed out the side door to the back of the porch. It was beautiful. Comfortable just in my t-shirt and sleep shorts.

Maybe my aunt had boxes and packing materials in the shed. I wandered with my coffee to the shed and peeked inside. Enough stuff to get started. A few boxes. Lots of trash bags. Not that I wanted to put any of her belongings into trash bags, but if it would save me a trip to the store on the moped ...

I went back inside and found packing supplies in the office and sharpies in the kitchen. I put my stash of stuff onto the floor in the library, and carefully pushed the couches to one side of the room. Now I had room to work.

I started with the books. Stacking them in piles. Most of the books went in the donate pile—they were just too heavy to ship and a lot of them were medical tomes. Some were bird-watching encyclopedias, and there were a number of novels. In the corner of the library, I found a collection of scrapbooks and photo albums. This was the stuff I was looking for.

By now I was ready for breakfast/ very late lunch. I grabbed the pile of scrapbooks and brought my empty coffee mug to the kitchen. I was tempted to pour just one more cup of coffee, but really, I had to stop the insanity of being up all night and asleep all day. No more caffeine. Peanut butter and jelly again. I made a mental note to head to the grocery store before it closed tonight.

I sat at the bar in the kitchen so I could see out the giant kitchen windows. It would be nice to eat in the kitchen nook once the new window was installed. I flipped through the photos in the albums. Aunt Del and Mom and their sister, Aunt Sally, growing up. I hadn't seen most of these pictures, probably because my aunt seemed to be the keeper of these albums, and not my mom. I had never been terribly close with my aunt Sally, maybe because my mom hadn't been. There hadn't been a falling out, just a falling away, it seemed. Then again, I had never asked about it; it was just how life had been. Sally had been stunning growing up. She had a natural smile and seemed to light up in front of the camera. I'd ask my mom some questions next time she called. I wondered if she had saved the cookies last night.

I cleared my dishes to the dishwasher and considered how to get groceries back to the house—even though I really didn't need all that much. Definitely milk for coffee, and breakfast, lunch, and dinner items. Well, maybe I did need a lot. Except that I should eat as much of the stuff at my aunt's house so I didn't need to throw it all away when I left. I flipped a page in my notebook and started another list, throwing open all the cabinet doors a second time.

There was a good number of shelf-stable items—mac and cheese, spaghetti, canned soups, even those canned fruit cocktails that I had when I was a kid. Remembering how I'd fight my brother for the one half-cherry when we opened the can, I smiled. Texted Mick a pic of the can. **I get the cherry**!

He immediately texted back. **I'll come. Next ferry.**

Don't worry. I got this.

Both my mom and brother wanted to come help me with my aunt's house. Both insisted on coming. But I told them it was something Aunt Del wanted me to do. If she had wanted me to do it with my brother or with my mom, then she wouldn't have left the job to me. Mick and Mom had respected my wishes and let me come alone.

When I was done listing all the food items and planned out meals, I realized I really didn't need much at the store. Fruit, milk, garlic, tomatoes, eggs, a couple of fresh items to round out the non-perishables. I eyed the cake mixes and thought that would be a fun thing to pop in the oven in between cleaning out the house. I wondered if there was a food pantry on the island for donating the rest of it.

Even though my work this morning felt scattered—kitchen work, shed work, back to the kitchen, I felt like I was on some sort of roll. Making good headway. I retreated to the library and sorted through the rest of the books, which was exhausting. I was ready to take a break and take a walk. Or a bike ride.

The bike I normally used when I came to visit was neatly lined up next to my aunt's in the shed. The tires were full and the bike looked ready to go. Maybe I'd kill a few birds: bike around the island and then stop at the grocery store on the way home. I ran back inside to grab my purse and the list. Thinking things through, I dumped out my purse onto the table in the foyer and sifted through all the things to find what I would need, and loaded it up into a small backpack in my aunt's closet. Easier to bike with a backpack than a purse.

In moments I was out in the warm spring afternoon, pedaling hard to get rid of the sifting-through-my-aunt's-stuff weariness. Instead of turning right at the first major intersection (not even a traffic light; just a stop sign—major seemed relative on the island), I turned left and followed the road until I hit the ocean, and then turned left again. I remembered taking this Oceanside Drive with my aunt on one of our bike rides—it circled the outskirts of the island and had the best views. If I went all the way around the island, I would eventually hit the bluffs, the south lighthouse, and circle back onto the main strip at the ferry dock and beach. My legs pumped and the sea air filled my lungs. For the first time, I felt like I had room to think. It almost felt like I *was* on vacation. Maybe I'd keep my aunt's house and rent it out. A week of this every year would be just what the doctor (my aunt) ordered.

Seagulls circled overhead and I pulled onto a sandy beach to watch them dive into the ocean. Rocks lined the shore. I made a mental note to bring tomorrow's PB and J sandwich here for a picnic. Straddling the bike, my head cleared and I felt energized to get back to work. But first, groceries. I checked my phone and saw that there was a store inland and on the north side of the island—a fairly long bike ride. Instead, I decided to turn around and bike into town and hit the general store. With my reduced shopping list, the general store had more than what I needed.

The ride was a nice one. At Island General, I found what I was looking for quickly, after spending a few minutes shoring up Tuesday's plan with Bells. The window was still slotted to come to the island on Friday and Bells said that she would head up the install herself.

I secured the groceries in the basket on the bike, with some stashed in my backpack, and turned toward my aunt's home in the light of the setting sun. I stopped whenever I saw something beautiful, so it was a leisurely ride back to the house. My phone was filling with gorgeous island shots at different vantage points. Waves crashing at the beach, sunset pics from the top of the hill, an egret nesting in the reeds near the shoreline rocks. A couple of my pictures were echoes of some of the framed photographs on the walls of my aunt's house. I made a mental note to mail those to myself. I'd love pictures of the island at my apartment in Boston.

Thinking about my real life, back on the mainland, gave me a really big reality check. Even if I came back here once a year for a week, it wasn't like that was enough to explore a relationship with Jesse. And even though we hadn't talked about that, it still wasn't fair to start something up that would go nowhere. Jesse had opened up to me in a way that felt much more like a relationship, and less like a one-night stand. I put the bike away in the shed, grabbed the groceries, and walked into the house, with a clearer head than I had since the storm.

I ignored the piles of sorted mess in my aunt's house and prepped a quick spaghetti dinner. Poured a glass of wine in an effort to get back onto the right sleeping timetable, ignoring that I had only been awake for six or so hours. From falling asleep out there yesterday, I knew it would be buggy on the deck at twilight. I sprayed bug spray on my arms and legs before balancing the dinner plate on a second photo album and taking my wine out to the back porch.

I flipped through the pictures in the fading light and wondered what my mom and aunts were thinking in each one. Family vacations, formal dances; normal kid-growing-up stuff.

And then I hit the hospital pictures. My mom had been in and out of the hospital as a teenager, with a chronic illness that ended in surgeries. As the youngest of the three, both her sisters were already away at college when things got rough. I saw lots of pictures of my aunt Del at her bedside; maybe that was when she decided to become a doctor.

My mom didn't talk about this time in her life very much. She just said things like, you never know what's going to happen tomorrow, so live a full day today; and when bad things happen, you never know who's going to step up and support you. She said she came out of that time with some very close friends. And she'd been lucky to be pretty healthy after the surgeries, so she had clearly closed the book on this part of her life.

I scrutinized the pictures, trying to infer as much as I could about the person my mom had been back then. In almost every picture, she was smiling, even when surrounded by doctors. Aunt Del was in a ton of the pictures, lying in bed curled up with my mom, playing board games on the hospital bed, lying on the cot beside the bed. Seeing in pictures how close they were, I wondered again why my aunt had given me the house. Wouldn't that be a better gift in the hands of my mom?

In the will, her big assets had been split evenly between my mom, myself, my brother, and my aunt Sally, who hadn't been available to go to the will reading. But I had gotten the house, and my aunt's money had gone to the other three. Which had struck me odd, then and now. My mom had just shrugged and said that Aunt Del always had her reasons.

I flipped to the end of the hospital section of the photo album and into the next vacation section of the book. Lots of pictures of my mom beaming and looking healthy again. Lots of pictures of her and Aunt Del together hugging and biking and hiking. But no pictures of Aunt Sally in this section. And now that I thought about it, there were no pictures of Aunt Sally in the hospital section at all. She had been at college like Aunt Del but clearly hadn't been able to come back to be with my mom.

In fact, it looked like that had been the moment of falling out. Lots of pictures of Aunt Sally before my mom got sick, but none during, and very few afterward. A few pictures of her at graduation from college, but other than that, it was as if she had fallen out of existence.

My phone rang. Thoughts of my family were so thick in my head, I assumed it was my mom calling back, finally, to let me know about the cookies. This time I checked before I blindly answered the call. It was Sheila from work. Wow. I hadn't thought about my work in a few days—even though I had told them and myself that I was on leave, I hadn't really believed I wouldn't work while on the island. I always worked.

"Hey, Sheila," I said as I picked up the call from my assistant.

"So sorry to bother you—I know you're dealing with family stuff, but the Salads For Everyone account is requesting a rebrand. They want it done by a week from Friday."

Eleven days to overhaul a brand from top to bottom and pitch it to a client? That was doable when I was in my office with my team, but while I was out on the island? Tough. But I wasn't one to shirk from a challenge. "Tell them yes, we'll do it."

"Do you want me to bring in Brian or someone?" I loved Brian, and he was a strong marketer, but I didn't need people from work poaching my clients. Except for Sheila, who I was training to take over projects herself one day.

"Nope, I got this. Can you set up an exploratory meeting with them tomorrow?"

"Sure. Exploratory zoom meeting Tuesday. Does one pm work?"

"Oh wait." Was tomorrow Tuesday? Bells was coming to help me sort through my aunt's stuff. And at the slow rate I was moving, I needed her to give me a boost. "Set the meeting for Wednesday at one pm. That way I can get a preliminary proposal going." Why were these words coming out of my mouth? A full day of sorting through my aunt's stuff and family memories AND a preliminary proposal in the next thirty hours? I guess I needed to get working. I put the wine glass down.

"Will do. I'll set up the virtual meeting and be there to take notes, as usual. I'll send you the link tomorrow."

"Thanks, Sheila, you're a lifesaver." What I really meant was I needed a lifesaver. I hoped Bells would be that for me tomorrow.

Well, the fantasy was officially over. Back to reality. Back to the fun work of marketing, the stress of deadlines, and all the stuff that went with the grind. I grabbed the Magic Eight Ball keychain to add some levity, but before I could ask it a question, the doorbell rang.

I hopped up to answer the door. It was a little late for visitors.

Jesse stood in the floodlight of the front porch light. Looking as sexy as ever. He ran his hand through his hair as usual and smiled at me, holding up a box tied with string. "Penny, from the cafe, sent this."

Seeing him suddenly after hours digging into family memories and the work phone call put him squarely in the right box—he was a fling, nothing more. I had been kidding myself by following these emotions and the attraction. My real life was off the island and doing the work I loved—marketing. I didn't have time for a long-distance thing, and it wasn't fair to him to lead him on. After what he shared with me last night, he clearly was looking for something more than a one-night stand.

Someone should tell my body that, though, because it reacted like it was a magnet to his presence and my skin longed for his touch all over my body. "Hey, Jesse. C'mon in." I'd be kind and firm, but let him know what was what. He deserved more than a fling. Plus, I really wanted to try whatever Penny had sent over for us.

I led him out to the porch where the photo albums were stacked up. I grabbed my wine glass. "Want a glass?"

"Wine would be great. Or beer." He settled into a lounge chair and all I wanted to do was settle in with him. Intertwine our bodies.

Instead, I headed into the bright lights of the yellow kitchen. "I'll take a look, but you might have to settle for wine."

I scoured the back of the fridge, as if a beer would magically appear, but there wasn't any to be found. I poured us both wine and steeled myself. I needed to stop acting like a teenager and I had to put a stop to this fling. I had to ignore the reaction I felt every time he was near. The electricity and warmth running through my body. *Stop it, Paige.* Oh. My. God. I needed to get a hold of myself.

Once I had cooled down enough that I felt like I could trust my reactions around him, I carried the glasses out on top of a plate with knives and forks for whatever delicacy was hiding in the cardboard box.

It was monkey bread—yum. Jesse had placed it center stage and was leafing through the photo albums. I cut the bread into pieces, wondering if it was supposed to be torn with our hands. But I didn't want to have sticky fingers, especially if we were looking at old photos of my family.

"These are cool images of your aunt growing up—I can spot her a mile away."

I handed him a plate of gooey bread and pushed the wine glass over. "How did you know her?" Anything to delay the inevitable.

"She helped my sister. She was a lovely person."

I pointed out some of my favorite shots of my mom and her sisters. I wasn't supposed to be getting closer to this man. "Look." I paused to take a giant bite of monkey bread. It dissolved in my mouth in gooey sweetness. Yum. "I'm sorry if I've led you on. The truth is I'm heading back to my life on the mainland as soon as I'm done settling my aunt's affairs. I'm selling the house and so the last thing I want to do is put down roots here."

I had made a clear decision. After all, my last relationship dissolved because of the long-distance thing. And Matt and I had been falling in love. It was best to shut this down now.

He stared at me in a way that unnerved me. Like he could see right through me. I wondered what exactly he saw. He took a sip of wine. "Have you put down roots anywhere?"

That was not the response I was expecting. "Excuse me?"

He waved his hand to encompass all the books on the table. "Don't you want this? Family? Love?"

"I do. Of course, I do. It just needs to fit in ..."

He had the gall to interrupt me. "Love doesn't fit in. When it happens—when you find that person you want to love and protect, you fit your life around that."

"That's easy for you to say."

"Easy for me to say?!" He stood up, angry. I hadn't seen him this way before. "You don't know the first thing about me."

"Exactly my point. I don't know you; you don't know me. Let's leave this here. I'll go back to my life on the mainland, sell my aunt's house, and you'll go back to your life here as if I never came."

"That sounds good to me. You don't know what it does to me to be here, at your aunt's house. As I said, you don't know the first thing about me. And it sounds like it might be better for me if it stays that way."

"What do you mean, it's hard for you to be here? Why?"

He downed the rest of the wine and walked away, following the porch around the house. Over his shoulder, he added, "You don't get to know—you've made it clear you don't want to be in my life."

I watched him disappear into the darkness and around the corner of the porch. I listened for his truck to rev up and drive away.

Well, that happened.

Even though he was mad, it was the right call. I was going back to my life; it was much better not to get attached. I dumped all the stuff from the porch into the kitchen, grabbed the wine bottle, the rest of the monkey bread, my wine glass, and headed up to bed. My aunt would certainly forgive me for eating and drinking in bed after that awful encounter. Even if I had to wash the monkey bread out of her sheets tomorrow.

Did I do the right thing? If I cared enough to find and shake my keychain it would probably say something stupid like: CANNOT PREDICT NOW

But that wasn't the only question I wanted to ask.

"Aunt Del, why did you leave me this house? Why didn't you leave it to one of your sisters?"

I listened to the house settling around me, the crickets in the bog, and the hoot of an owl echoing in the night.

I didn't get an answer to my questions.

7

I got up when the dark turned into a slightly rosy glow. I hadn't slept much, but I had eaten all the monkey bread and drank all the wine. Determination was going to have to get me through my day. I had to finish the house stuff so I could make an appointment with the realtor to take photos and start the selling process. All before my work meeting tomorrow. I pushed all thoughts of Jesse and that awful encounter from my mind. Or, tried to.

I was dressed and coffee-ed and feeling at least human enough to open the door for Bells when she arrived at nine am.

She handed me another cup of coffee and a muffin from the cafe. "Thought we'd start off the day on the right foot. Or, the right bite."

I waved her in and looked out onto the beautiful spring day, unseasonably warm for New England. "I'm going to gain a million pounds if I eat Penny's food every day." I took a huge bite as I walked her into the mess of the house. "But it will be worth it; this is amazing!" Lemon poppyseed, my favorite.

"Okay, here is what I was thinking: we'll sort through everything today and then go out tonight, for girls' night. I have tomorrow off from the store as well—it's like today is my Saturday. So, let's do it right. I brought boxes."

Oh, thank goodness. Bells was all about taking the lead, so I let her. Quickly, she had moving boxes out, folded together, and labeled. Her whirlwind of movement reassured me that even after the series of sleepless nights, I would get it all done, with her help.

We started in the library—again. We worked quietly and efficiently. I felt energized by her movement and quiet work ethic. As we were placing the fiftieth medical book in the donate box, she said, "I bet people would love some of this stuff. You know, everyone loved your aunt."

I could see an idea sprouting behind her eyes.

"What if, instead of hauling this all to the donation center or recycling center, we have a give-away day here, at her house. Invite everyone to come and take something to remember your aunt by?" She paused, dropped another book in a box, and took a sip of her coffee. "Actually, what if we take it one step further? Hold a sort of life celebration party?"

It was probably the jolt of yummy cafe coffee, but I allowed myself to get infected by Bells' enthusiasm. "We didn't really know who to reach out to on the island for Aunt Del's service, so yeah, you guys didn't really get to join in."

"Well, we had a party at Magnolias, to honor her. And her coworkers did a remembrance at the hospital. But this would be super fun. We could have an outside party, if the weather holds, and set up the things we're donating on shelves, and string lights, and ..." Bells got lost in her thoughts and I smiled.

The idea just seemed so right. So perfect. So Aunt Del.

The rest of the day flew by. It was easier to plow through things with a fun party to look forward to once the work was done at the end of the week. I made lunch for both of us trying to use as many ingredients from the kitchen as possible, using an app that told me what to make from the ingredients on hand. It wasn't up to Penny's standards, for sure, but it was edible. Bells took it all in stride and made it super fun.

By the time she said goodbye before dinner, telling me to "pretty-up" for our night out, I was happy but exhausted. I decided not to do my normal thing of spending way too much time on work and just took a few minutes to sketch out the new branding for my client that I had thought of during the day. Done and done.

I showered, blew my hair out, and applied fun makeup—glitter eye-liner I hadn't ever used before and bright eye shadow. I generally thought of make-up as a tool to make me look more professional for work, but tonight I wanted to impress Bells and experiment a bit. And she had told me to *pretty-up.* And I loved the way it felt to get pretty for me, not for work, and not for a guy.

My thoughts turned to Frank, and I wondered if he had gotten the message to leave me alone. I pushed those musings aside; Frank wasn't going to ruin a night of pure fun! And then, of course, I thought of Jesse. But that was not happening. Not. Happening.

I biked my way to the bar, knowing that my low tolerance with drinks and the moped wouldn't mix, and locked it up at the bike stand in the parking lot in the back. When I walked inside, Bells was already there with two women, Margo, and someone I didn't know. They yelled my name as I went in, and I grinned widely. It was the first time I had ever had a Cheers-like response. Going out with friends after work had never felt this enjoyable—it had felt like networking, to be honest. Everyone guarded and trying to seem sophisticated.

I ran over and Margo handed me a drink. "Rum and ginger beer, right?"

"Anything with ginger beer is my favorite!"

"I've put that in the bartender's vault." She tapped the blond curls on her head. "Moscow Mule, Anejo High Ball, Gin Gin Mule, or oh, the El Diablo. We can have fun with those! Good drinks. Good island drinks. We can pretend we're in the Mediterranean!"

"I'll drink to that! Oh, we should take a girls' cruise sometimes. I'm a sucker for all those souvenir glasses you get at cruise bars." Bells took a deep sip of her drink.

"She is," the new girl piped up. "You should see the weirdness on her shelves. A Pufferfish drink glass, a coconut drink glass, a disco ball drink glass. Hi, Paige, I'm Nellie. Nice to meet you!"

I shook her hand and she pulled me into a hug.

"I keep telling Margo to offer a collection of collective drink glasses here, but she won't take it to her brother."

"We own this bar together. And, maybe this year, I can push for that, Bells. We just don't know that it will be cost-effective."

"Cool, you own this place?" I looked at the bar in a new light. I'd never known someone who owned their own restaurant or bar before.

I took a sip. It was so good. I was having fun, fun like I hadn't had in years. I hadn't even realized that I hadn't been having fun in my life on the mainland. Bells had already been more supportive than friends I'd had for years. Willing to help me sort through my aunt's stuff on her day off. And inviting me out with her friends. I had only met her a few days ago. For some reason, thinking about my new but weirdly deep friendship with Bells made me think about what Jesse said last night about molding one's life around love. And it made me think of Cynthia, who I only met through my breakup with Frank. Was friendship supposed to hit like lightning? It hadn't been my experience before, but I liked it. I liked that feeling of sudden closeness.

"Do you all not have work tomorrow?" Because at the rate we were sipping our drinks, tomorrow was going to be a questionable day.

"I work, but not until noon. Nellie is a teacher, but she doesn't believe in hangovers."

"True. I alternate drinks with water and make sure I'm hydrated. My English classes will not be the wiser tomorrow."

"One day, that's going to bite you in the butt, you know." Margo flipped a finger toward the guy behind the bar who nodded. Another round.

Bells looked at her vibrating phone. "Looks like I'm going to test that theory—Jesse texted, asking that I give him a hand at his place tomorrow."

Jesse's name brought back the image of him walking away last night, but this time, with a drink in my belly and no dinner yet, I just enjoyed the mental image. His backside was very taut. I probably should feel other things—like bummed out that I wasn't going to explore his hands all over my body—but I had decided to have a good night and that was that. No room for being bummed.

"What will you do at his house?"

"He's building a house himself over near Blaire's Bluff. He had to get a variance from the island board to do it—no new buildings are usually permitted. But he wow-ed them with his designs and they finally gave him the go-ahead. He's doing it mainly by himself, in between construction work through the general store and his work on the emergency response crew. I don't know what we're doing tomorrow—he's all framed out but not much further along."

"Wow." I didn't know he was that capable—to build a house by himself? It just reinforced how little I knew about him in general. "Impressive."

"Oh my gosh, you have no idea. He planned to build that house for his sister—she was sick most of her life and her dream was to have a house with bluff views. But it took too long for the island to pass the permit. Island bureaucratic red tape. So sad. Now he's building it to sell. Breaks my heart."

A tray of drinks hit the table, and I gave Margo's brother the once over. And then the twice over. Did this island only produce hot guys? *Way to objectify, Paige.* I needed some food, stat, as my aunt would say.

"Hey, thanks, bro. Can we order some dinner?"

"Sure, what can I get you guys?"

"Paige, this is Drew, my brother." Margo nodded at him while passing out the drinks.

"Delilah's niece, right?"

"Shush, Drew, she might not want to talk about her aunt." She rolled her eyes and mouthed "I'm sorry" in my direction.

"No, no, that's fine! I'm fine." I sipped the yummy new drink. "Yup, Del was my aunt." I decided to float Bells' idea to the girls. "We're thinking of holding a party to celebrate her life at her house, and everyone can take something of hers to remember her by."

"Oh, so cool. I bet we can donate some wine and champagne." Margo looked pointedly at her brother, who rolled his eyes. Clearly a lot of their communications were conveyed through eye-rolling.

"It's a miracle we clear any profit at all here, with my sister's big heart."

"Oh, I can totally pay for it."

"No, no. We loved Del. Margo's right. We'd be happy to give you a couple of cases of wine and champagne. When were you thinking?"

Bells answered before I could get my planning gears working. "Either Friday or Saturday; whenever Penny can fill the food order."

Oh my gosh, this was happening. And fast.

"Sounds great. Maybe we can drop off the cases on Thursday when I do my weekend deliveries at the restaurants. Does that work?"

Before I could say that this was moving way too quickly, Bells responded again, "Perfect. Thank you so much!"

"So, food orders. Go. I know you'll have the loaded taters, Bells. Margo—a salad?" At Margo's nod, Drew continued. "Nellie, what will it be tonight?"

"How about some appetizers to share. Dealer's choice."

"Perfect. And, Paige?"

"Do you have some soft pretzel bites or something?" By far, my favorite bar food.

"Oh, we have the best huge soft pretzels. Yum," Margo answered.

"Alright, have a fun girls' night."

"Thanks, Drew. Appreciate it!"

After he had gone back behind the bar to plug the order into the computer system, Bells leaned in. "He always says it's Margo with the big heart, but he's just a big softie. He would have offered to donate that stuff if she hadn't."

"You all are the best." It wasn't the drinks talking; I meant it.

★★★

I was having such a fun time at the bar, but it was more than that —I was sharing more with these women than I had shared in a really long time. Mental note: Be more open with my friends at home.

The food arrived and we passed along the hors d'oeuvres around. The pretzel was bigger than my plate so we laughed and passed that along as well. Bells punched Margo lovingly on the arm after they joked about something. I couldn't stop comparing this night with nights out back at home. I couldn't honestly picture my Boston friend group being this easy to hang with. Cynthia was the only one who would fit in with this vibe. I had been spending my time thinking this was the vacation and the mainland was my reality, but maybe I could make my reality more like this—people who cared about me relaxing together. Sometimes perspective and time away from things helped me to see what was true.

We ate and drank and then moved over to a pool table. Every once in a while, I hit a decent shot, but mostly, I was the butt of the pool jokes. Laughter came easily. I tried to figure out exactly how my life on the mainland had become about work and nothing else. I loved my work, but I used that perspective as a reason to not care that I didn't have many deep friends in my life. Cynthia for sure, but that was really it. And I had only known her a few months. And Matt, but he had moved away in January. I tried to stop thinking and just enjoy the moment, but my mind just kept running back to why my life didn't feel more like this on the mainland.

My pool cue completely slid off the white ball and it bounced against the side of the table, not hitting any other balls.

"Scratch! Drink!" Bells yelled to me.

I downed the rest of the drink and Margo yelled, "Drew, put some drinks in our hands!"

He rolled his eyes and nodded from behind the bar.

Nellie lined up her next shot and sunk two balls in one clean motion.

I continued comparing this night with past nights in Boston. Frank loved to show me off but didn't like me to go to bars without him. He hadn't started out controlling my life; it had been a slow build. He had just gotten more and more anxious about our relationship. Which was totally incompatible with the way I had wanted to live my life—passionate about Frank, yes, but also fully immersed in work and good friends. But I had still been willing to try to make it work until I came home to him banging someone else. And then I had ended it. And I had become good friends with his mistress, which is totally weird, but those sorts of things happened to me. I wondered what Cynthia would think about Jesse. I know she would love Bells and Margo and Nellie.

Nellie finished off the game with quiet finesse, and we sat back down at the table.

"I'm going to eat the rest of this huge pretzel unless you guys help me!" I passed my plate around.

"So, Paige." Margo leaned in conspiratorially, even though she was talking so loudly, I was sure people on the beach could hear. "You and Jesse. An item?"

Oh boy. I didn't know how to answer.

"Um, he's really nice ..."

"Nice?" Nellie giggled and I had a feeling her English class would see a hangover tomorrow. "That's not the first word I'd use to describe Jesse. Hot?"

"Nells, he is so nice, though. Paige is right." Bells defended both me and Jesse.

"We just, well, I just decided that I couldn't lead him on. After all, I'm going back to Boston in a few days—and long-distance rarely works."

Bells gestured dismissively. "But do you feel *all the things* when he's around? Why do you have to make it all about what's going to work in the future—enjoy him now! I would."

Margo shook her head. "Not all of us are like you, Bells, ready to have a good time with any riff-raff the ferry brings to the island."

"They aren't riff-raff, Margo. They're fun. And that's my point."

"I don't think that would be fair to him." I was sobering up quickly. Luckily Drew brought another round to the table. If this interrogation was going to last, I'd need some liquid courage. I took a long sip.

"Why don't you let him decide that? After all, he's not planning on staying on this island forever."

"No?" That seemed to be news to Nellie. "Jack's good friends with Jesse." Nellie explained to me, "Jack's my guy. He hasn't mentioned that Jesse is thinking of moving. Margo, has he said anything to you?"

"Um, Bartender/Stool Sitter confidentiality." She laughed. "But, no, he hasn't."

"He hasn't *said* anything to me either, but it's just the way he is when he works on his house. That house was supposed to be for his sister, he was so excited about it, and then when she passed ... well, it's a whole different thing. I think it will be too painful for him to stay. Oh my god, this is my favorite song!"

I wanted to ask what had happened, exactly, with his sister, but Margo was right about respecting him—if Jesse had wanted to open up to me, he would have. After all, he hadn't spread word around town about me wandering out into the rain and slipping stupidly like a city girl. I didn't need to pry with my new friends. I let the chatter from the girls about the music wash over me. But had I given him the chance to open up? If he wasn't planning on living on this island forever, then was I wrong in not giving this thing a chance? Maybe. Maybe I should have been more open to him. Hearing that he was building a whole house for his sister gave me something else to consider about him, and also made me think of my own brother. Mick and I were super close too; I couldn't imagine losing him so young like Jesse lost his sister. I felt a compassionate stab to my heart as I considered what that would feel like. I wondered what Mick would think about Jesse? The drinking was making my mind wander in all sorts of directions.

Bells pulled me out on the "dance" floor and we all swayed a little and watched Margo let loose. She twirled around, grabbing patrons up from their seats until we had a whole crowd grooving to the music.

When the song died out, we all waited to see what the next pick on the jukebox would be and it was nothing ... silence. We all looked at each other and laughed, and went back to our table. Nellie grabbed a pitcher of water from Drew and refilled our glasses. "You'll thank me in the morning, ladies! And on that note, I have to go—school starts early tomorrow!"

I tried to pay the bill, but Bells had already settled the tab. "You can pick it up next time!"

"But you worked all day at my aunt's—the least I can do is pay for your dinner and drinks."

"It was my turn—we can't let the new person pay! We'll fold you into the rotation. You can be next."

"I'll be next." Having a next time out with these women sounded amazing. I hoped I'd be able to fit another night out before I headed back to my real-life next weekend.

Margo stayed to help her brother out, but Bells, Nellie, and I walked out together. I pulled on a sweater against the cold and grabbed my bike.

"See you all later," Bells yelled as she and Nellie headed in different directions on foot.

"See you!" I straddled the bike and started off down the road to my aunt's house. I was doing fine until I turned the corner onto my aunt's street too widely and ended up hitting a giant rock in the sandy shoulder. The bike stopped but I kept going and landed on my side with the bike on top off me. Luckily, I landed in the sand and not on the road. Stupid idea: biking while drunk!

I dusted myself off and checked for cuts and scrapes. Seeing nothing, I inspected the bike. Somehow, I had mangled the front of the bike and it was unsuitable to ride. I walked the bike the rest of the way, hoping (just a little) that someone with a truck might come and rescue me and share a deep kiss.

I dropped the bike on the front lawn, full-on in vacation fantasy mode, imagining his hands on my body while I climbed the stairs and sank into bed.

If Jesse showed up right now, would I invite him in and ravish him? I imagined the Magic Eight Ball telling me: IT IS DECIDEDLY SO.

8

I awoke in a puddle of sunshine. I groggily got up and staggered over to the bedroom window, opened the glass, and smiled out at the sunny day. The distant ocean sounds and the call of seagulls washed over me while the crisp salty air rejuvenated me.

If I was going to host a party at the house, I had a lot of work to do. I made a mental list: gather all the things that Bells and I had decided were trash and take them to the recycling center near the dock, get tables and chairs to set up outside, along with decorations. All before my work meeting at one pm.

I pulled out the napkin Bells had given me last night with the name and number of a guy with a truck on the island—Xavier, I thought I might have already met him at the bar, but couldn't quite remember. I called and was sure I had the wrong number— the man on the other end was gruff and short with me. But by the end of the call, he had said yes, he'd come and pick me up to drop things at the recycling center and pick up tables and chairs I was renting from the general store.

I quickly brewed coffee, added milk, yum, and threw together a peanut butter and jelly sandwich. I pulled all the black trash bags from yesterday's sorting out onto the gravel driveway. My aunt's bike was mangled and lying in the yard where I had left it last night. It was definitely more bent than I thought it should be. I considered adding it to the trash pile, but that seemed wasteful. It was a good bike; I'd just have to add "find a bike mechanic" to the list of things I needed to do before I left. I toasted another piece of bread and just added jelly to it—I was still hungry and didn't know whether I'd have time to make lunch before the work meeting.

Xavier was right on time and a tad impatient. He honked the horn as he drove up my aunt's drive. I rushed out to point at the trash pile, and he didn't wait for me to help. He threw everything into the truck bed and shook his head when I said I needed to grab a jacket and my purse from the house. I rushed, spilled my coffee, and upended my jelly toast all over the entranceway. I cleaned up the coffee as best as I could while Xavier pounded on the truck's horn. Rude. I'd have to clean it properly when I got back. I ran back out to the truck and tried to smooth things over.

"Thank you so much for doing this! I appreciate it."

"I'm not doing it for free, you know." If he hadn't been so grumpy, he would have been really hot. Well, he was kinda hot anyway.

"Oh, I didn't mean to imply you were. It's just ..." Yeah, that was all I had. If he was going to stew, he could stew. It was a beautiful day and I wasn't going to let his bad mood ruin my excitement.

He pushed a white bag into my lap as we turned out of Aunt Del's driveway. "My mom packed that and told me to give you one."

"Your mom?"

"Penny. We own the diner."

"Penny's your mom?" I tried not to sound incredulous. Maybe Xavier was just having a rough day and he was normally as outgoing as his mom. I tried to give him the benefit of the doubt. I pulled a pastry from the bag and bit in. Yup, I was going to weigh 400 pounds at the end of this trip. And it was totally worth it.

We dropped off the trash at the recycling center, and Bells loaded the rental stuff into the truck at the general store, all bubbly about invitations she had posted all around the island about the celebration at my aunt's. It was coming together quickly. She also loaded a ton of Edison-bulb string lights. "They'll be so perfect when the sun goes down, fairy-like!" I smiled and started to get excited again about the party. Outdoor lights were my favorite.

Xavier smiled at Bells' enthusiasm and once we left town, he turned to me, a new kind of grimace on his face. "Hey, look. I'm sorry about your aunt. She was the best."

I nodded. It meant something to me that everyone I met loved my aunt. Even this guy of few words. We unloaded the supplies from the truck and I waved him goodbye. He grinned and waved back at me.

I left everything in a pile on the front lawn; it was time to start my virtual work meeting. As I was booting up the laptop, I wondered where the bike had gone—Xavier and I had plunked everything down in the exact spot I had abandoned my bike the night before. I didn't have time to investigate, and I hoped it hadn't ended up in the trash pile after all.

I quickly clicked on the meeting link and waved to Sheila. We chatted and checked in before the client came into the virtual call. Instead of laying out my plan right away, I gave the client time to talk about their new needs and why they were changing gears. I loved the direction they wanted to go in and asked question after question to get more info on that new direction. Then I started to lay out my plan and schedule for the new campaign.

"So, I'll change some things on my end, but I also want to know from you what you think *worked* from the first campaign." The front door of the house banged open and Jesse's voice frantically yelled out, "Paige, Paige, are you okay?" Oh my god, what was happening?

I smiled awkwardly into the camera, and quickly excused myself, "I'll be back in a moment—why don't you tell us what was working, and Sheila, would you mind taking extra-detailed notes?" Not waiting for a reply, I muted my computer and ran into the kitchen, where Jesse met me and grabbed me up into his arms.

"You're alright? You're alright!"

I hugged him back fiercely. "I'm fine! What's going on?"

He sank into a kitchen stool and put his head in his hands. "I'm sorry. I must look like a crazy person. I saw your mangled bike on the lawn, but you weren't at home; I thought the worst. I grabbed it and threw it into my truck and have been combing the island for you. I went to the hospital and to urgent care. Couldn't find you anywhere." I pushed a glass of water into his hand and he lifted his head. "I'm so sorry. Clearly, I was panicked about nothing. You're okay. I'll leave." He saw the computer open and the meeting going forward without me and jumped up to go.

I grabbed his long-sleeved shirt in my hand and held onto it. "Hold on a second."

Unmuting the computer, I waved at the clients and Sheila. "Let's take five, while I deal with something." At their nods, I turned off the video and muted my microphone again.

"I don't want you to leave. I'm sorry I scared you." I pulled him back into a hug and pressed my body to his. "I think I made a mistake."

"It wasn't your fault I overreacted. I'm sorry. I'm a little jittery these days about people I care about. I heard what you said the other night and I don't want to be the guy who doesn't get it—that guy that hangs on, that guy that ..."

"No, I mean, I think I made a mistake when I said we shouldn't pursue this ..." Enough words. I wanted to *show* him what I meant.

I kissed him, hard, pressing my mouth to his, in part because I couldn't stand being this close without tasting him, and in part to stop him from talking.

"Who are *you*?" A voice came from my aunt's open door. A voice I recognized, a voice I honestly hoped never to hear again. I groaned into Jesse's mouth, and not the good groan that says let's-take-this-upstairs, but the bad groan that says omg-my-ex-is-in-the-doorway-and-thank-god-I-turned-off-my-work-camera-because-things-are-about-to-get-messy. And, not good messy.

I wanted to ignore Frank. I wanted to pretend he wasn't there and dig into this kiss. But Jesse's body jerked away from mine and I knew, without even looking, that Frank had his hands on Jessie. This was not going to end well.

"Get your hands off of Paige." Frank had Jesse by the arm. Jesse shook him off, his eyes narrowing. I would have sworn the testosterone crackled in the air.

I got between them and placed one hand on each of their chests. Jesse cocked his head, sizing up this stranger. He pushed Frank back and grabbed me around the waist and pulled me to his side.

"Frank, what are you doing here?" I wanted to put myself between the two again, but I also wanted to keep Jesse's hands on me, pulling me into him. I split the difference and put my arms out between them, but inched in closer to Jesse. He might have taken that slightly wrong and angled his body between mine and Frank's in a protective stance. I didn't need protection against my ex; he was harmless.

I heard the meeting start up again without me. I was really glad Sheila and my clients couldn't see or hear what was happening in my aunt's kitchen. But it was really distracting. I should be dealing with work; not with these two guys that seemed on the verge of a fistfight.

Frank ignored my question.

"I'm only going to say it one more time: Get your hands off of Paige."

"And you are?" Jesse's voice was so calm, and yet I could hear the edge underneath.

"I have an idea!" I tried to muster up my most peppy impression of Bells. "Let's grab a few beers, I mean, wine—I don't have any beers—and take this out to the porch. I can finish my work meeting and you guys can meet. Jesse, this is my ex, Frank. Frank, this is my, um, well ..." I turned into Jesse without letting him loosen his grip. "Please forgive me for what I said the other night. I want to explore this." Which would have been a much sexier sentence had I not said it within spitting distance of my ex. Oh, and a work meeting.

Jesse pulled my front to his front and took my face in both of his hands as if we were the only people in the world. "Forgiven and forgotten. Take your meeting. Do what you need to do. Don't worry about us. You and I will talk after." I hoped we would do more than just talk. An incentive for getting out of this mess quickly.

I pulled away to grab some wine glasses, but Jesse pulled me back into his arms, and kissed me deeply and thoroughly, maybe just to mark his territory in front of the other male in the room, but I didn't care. It felt so right. Electricity zapped through my body and I felt like I could accomplish anything.

"I'll grab the wine and glasses. I've got this—you do your work call. Frank—let's go." Jesse pointed to the back door.

"This isn't over." Frank seethed in the kitchen and acted as if he wasn't going anywhere.

"Seriously, Paige, go to your meeting. We're good."

Frank seemed the opposite of good, but I grabbed my laptop anyway and scurried to the stairs. "I'll be back down in two seconds." I shut the still-open front door and paused on the bottom step. Wavering if leaving them alone was the right thing to do at this moment.

"Please take your time, we'll behave. Right, Frank?"

I didn't wait to see what Frank's response was. I trusted Jesse. I took the stairs two at a time and settled into the desk in the master bedroom, clicked the camera back on, and flipped off the mute setting.

"Hey everyone, I'm sorry. I'm officially on leave, trying to settle my aunt's affairs. But you are such important clients, I took this meeting anyway. I'm sorry that I've wasted so much of your time today!"

"It's been the opposite, actually, not a waste of time at all. Sheila has a brilliant take on the project."

"Oh, no. I just followed Paige's lead—these are all her notes I'm working from."

A week ago, I would have let Sheila undermine herself because it was the way things normally worked. Because what she said was true, she was elaborating on my new direction. But now, I was starting to feel as though the collaboration was more important than taking credit for my ideas—Sheila was brilliant, and if I give her a little more agency, she would rise to the challenge. Just as the party for the islanders at my aunt's house was an idea I never could have come up with and implemented on my own—maybe that kind of magic could happen with my advertising clients too. To hell with how the firm normally worked. Sheila could breathe new life into this project and a fresh perspective.

"Sheila has an amazing eye for design and getting an emotional response from campaigns—I'd love to hear more of her own ideas, and I think it would benefit your campaign as well. Why don't I turn the meeting officially over to her and she can fill me in later?" I didn't hear any fighting from downstairs, but this would let me make sure things didn't end with someone in the hospital.

"You're in great hands with Sheila." I ignored Sheila shaking her head the tiniest (but fiercest) bit. Meanwhile, I texted her: **You got this! Just forward me the notes!**

"Thanks for taking our call on your vacation. Where does this leave our forward motion with the new campaign?"

"Sheila will take the lead and work on getting the proposal and visuals to you by the end of next week. Does that work? Best of both worlds. You get my expertise, but also new perspective from Sheila." I ignored Sheila's text reply: **Noooooo I'm not ready**.

"Again, you're in great hands. At our next meeting, Sheila will be the lead, and I will be her back-up." I signed off the call and shut the laptop. I quickly texted her affirmations to make sure she knew she could do this.

Three days on the island, one girls' night out, and a bunch of super-kisses from Jesse and I was feeling like superwoman.

I sighed and walked back downstairs. There was no sign of the men, but Jesse had left me a large glass of wine on the counter. Something in the back of my head said I should probably eat something since my jelly toast was still wallpapering the foyer, but the quiet worried me.

Was the testosterone getting the best of them? If I bothered to shake my Eight Ball, it would probably say: ALL SIGNS POINT TO YES.

9

I eased out the back door and onto the deck, wine glass in hand. Jesse stood in front of me at the deck's railing, looking out at the bog, his body relaxed, sipping his drink.

Frank stood facing the door, with his hands crossed across his chest, his empty wine glass discarded on the glass table, an alarmingly red patch on his face around his eye. He dabbed his nose with a napkin, and I could see some blood. "Paige. Tell this guy to get lost so we can talk."

Jesse turned to me, shook his head, and rolled his eyes. "Don't be a dick."

That, and Frank's developing black eye, summarized what I had missed.

"Did you?" I looked at Jesse.

"I didn't want to. But he came at me." Jesse shook his head. "Do you need us to leave so you can get back to your meeting?"

"You're dating a psycho, Paige. A psycho." Frank said, while cowered in the corner of the deck, glaring at Jesse.

When I tried to approach Frank to look at his eye, he put up his hand and shook his head. "It's nothing. I don't even feel it." He spat the words at Jesse.

"Look, dick, get your head out of your ass and see what Paige is going through here. She's grieving her aunt. When you love someone, you take care of them. Unless they tell you otherwise. Paige has been clear with you. You're just too self-absorbed to realize it." He downed the rest of his wine. "Paige, can I remove this guy from your aunt's house?"

I blinked. Two men stood before me: Jesse searching my face to try to read what he should do next. He would do whatever I wanted him to do; he was clearly giving me time to figure out what that was. And Frank shying away from Jesse, not caring about what I wanted or needed; here for his own agenda.

But, did either of them see me? The true me? I knew Frank didn't; he kept doing the opposite of what I asked. And Jesse seemed to see me, but was it just that we were both grieving people we loved? Was that enough to build a relationship on? And did I even care? I didn't know the answers of these questions, and it felt too important to ask the Magic Eight Ball. But I did know that I wanted Frank out of my aunt's house, out of my life permanently.

If I gave Frank even the smallest encouragement, he would start inserting himself back into my life, and that wasn't healthy for me. By the end of our relationship, he had driven all of my friends away with his controlling behavior. The short relationship with Matt after breaking up with Frank let me know that I didn't have to be in a bad relationship.

I didn't think Frank had acted that way on purpose. It was a product of his own anxiety, but he hadn't gotten help or changed his ways, and I just couldn't live with it anymore. Deep down I grieved the Frank I had fallen in love with, but if he wasn't going to behave in respectful ways, there wasn't anything I could do about it. About him. I deserved someone who was my best friend, not someone who made me feel like I needed to change to be loved.

"You. Stay here." I smiled sweetly at Jesse.

"You. I'll walk you out." I gestured to Frank to head back through the house with me. I still felt a bit of a high for finishing up the work call on the right note. For not offering to drop everything I was doing at my aunt's house to plan a whole new marketing campaign, and for finally giving my assistant the room to take the lead.

I waited until I slid the deck door shut before starting the conversation.

"What are you doing here?" I maneuvered him through the kitchen.

"I needed to see you." His voice, which had been stern, suddenly was sweet. The old Frank whom I used to love. He dabbed at his nose. I resisted the urge to get him some ice as we passed the refrigerator. I didn't want him to misinterpret any kindness.

"We've been broken up for months, why now?" We walked through the foyer, and I opened the front door; momentum was my plan when it came to Frank.

"Look, it was all a mistake. I just need you back. That's why." He leaned his back against the door until it closed and we were facing each other.

I tried not to think about how much I wanted to go and explore things with Jesse. All the things. In the short walk away from Jesse, I decided that even if we were just helping each other get over grief, I wanted that right now. Jesse made me feel better. And that was enough. But, right now, I needed to be firm with Frank and end this for good. He had come all the way out to the island to find me.

"Wait, Frank, how did you find me?"

"I called your mom."

"You called my mom? And she told you where I was?" It felt like a betrayal. I hoped those cookies from the other night had burnt to a crisp.

"Well, she didn't at first—she knew we had broken up. But listen. That's all in the past." He reached out to grab my arms, but I stepped back. "I'm sorry. Please forgive me. I need you."

"I have forgiven you." And as I said the words, I knew it was true. I had forgiven him. For the affair, for everything. I had let it all go. Moved on. Thanks in no small part to my other ex, Matt. "But forgiven or not, I don't want to get back together." I watched his face go from desperate to stony. A chill went down my spine. "But I can be here for you as a friend."

His tone changed as well. From sweet to, well, not sweet. "We have to get back together. I can't do this without you." His voice was quiet, but angry. So angry. This was a side of him I had never seen before. He had been anxious and controlling, sure, but never angry. Even when we were arguing, he was always so relaxed—probably because he knew he'd get his way. I'd always let him get his way. And when we broke up, I tried to make it a clean break. But he had kept trying to get me back—he had even proposed to me at my aunt's wake. Which was unacceptable on so many levels.

I took another step back. I made my voice super calm. "Do what? You can't do what?"

"My mom died." His eyes filled with pain. "Suddenly. Out of nowhere."

"Oh no, I'm so sorry." I put my wine glass down on the edge of the stairs and took him into my arms. That explained everything. All his behavior. He was grieving in his own way. "I didn't know."

"See, this is what I needed."

"You can have this from me. I'll always be here for you." I held him a moment longer and then it was like a switch clicked. He untangled us.

"That's what I needed to know."

Abruptly, he turned, opened the door, and left without so much as a goodbye or a wave of his hand. What had just happened? The door closed behind him. I had whiplash from the emotional ride. Stern to sweet to angry to sad to out-of-the-door, all within the space of two minutes.

"Well, he never was the most emotionally solid of people," I told the closed door. I wondered if I should unblock him from my phone, should I be there for him? A Magic Eight Ball response popped into my head: OUTLOOK NOT SO GOOD. I shrugged, grabbed my glass of wine, and did a mental tally of the day.

Trash to the recycling center. Supplies picked up. Work meeting: done. Ex, gotten rid of. Kind of. And my prize? The very kind, very interesting, very good-looking guy on my porch. I took a sip of wine and walked through the kitchen. I could get caught up in the tornado of Frank, or I could let him go and focus on what was going right. Because if I took Frank out of the equation, then it was like everything was coming up Paige today.

Sliding open the back door, I joined Jesse at the railing. I put one arm around him and pulled him sideways until we were literally joined at the hip. "Sorry about all that."

"No, I'm sorry. I came in like a crazy person and turned your day upside-down. And then your ex …. Well, he's a piece of work. Now that he's gone, I'm happy to leave and give you some peace."

"No, I'm totally the one who should be sorry—I think we're good for each other, for the moment, anyway." And I wanted to add that maybe it was good that he physically put Frank in his place. Since all Frank was doing was ignoring my boundaries. But I thought maybe that wasn't a stance I should take.

"I can see why you're hesitant—Frank is a dick."

And for some reason, I wanted to defend my ex. His mother had just died after all—we were all grieving. Frank just did it differently.

"We really seemed to fit in the beginning. And then one day I looked at my life, and all I had was him and arguments all the time. My work-life was great, but all the time outside of work was devoted to trying to keep him happy. I didn't know where all my friends had gone. Something needed to give. I honestly thought I'd give it another chance, though, and then, I caught him cheating. So, you know, it's been completely over for a few months. I even dated a nice guy after I broke it off with him." At his concerned look, I reassured him. "That's over too. Matt moved to

Texas. He showed me that sometimes the best things are things we don't plan. I do miss him. He told me if Frank pulled anything to give him a call." But of course, I didn't. Because he was all the way in Texas.

"And here I was, popping up all over the place. You even told me I seemed like a stalker." His voice was wistful, sadder than his words should have been.

"No, no. I mean, all of this is a little confusing, but in a very good way. Don't compare this with my relationship with Frank—I don't." Now that I was ready to let us comfort each other, I was ready to do some comforting. I faced him and ran my hand up his arm to his shoulder.

He turned to face me, too. His eyes looked lost and I wanted to help.

"Hey, what's going on?" I put my wine glass down on the railing and held his shoulders in both my arms.

"I don't want to dump on you—you're dealing with a lot. I should go. This day isn't about me."

I turned and stared into the bog considering his words. I *was* dealing with a lot. My aunt's death and being in charge of her things, not to mention that being on the island gave me perspective to examine what my life had become. And I wanted to examine that life. I was finally seeing that I had allowed my life to become a certain way and I wanted to start choosing my life rather than letting other people to choose my life for me—like Frank. I had turned my life around for Frank while we were together. I was as much to blame for my life turning into something I didn't want. Matt had helped teach me that I needed to start choosing what I wanted. The question was, did I want Jesse? Maybe just to help us both get over our losses. A bird flew over the bog. For the first time in a long time, I felt like I was like a bird —that I could choose to fly wherever I wanted to go. And if I wanted to fly smack into this guy I had just met, and throw caution to the wind, I could.

"That's true, I'm dealing with a lot. But I see you here, in front of me, and you're hurting. And I like the connection we made. I'm willing to choose to see where this will lead. So, I want to know why you're hurting. Especially since you've seen why I'm hurting —my aunt and the relationship with Frank—and you're still here. So, talk to me."

I turned back to him.

He stared into the bog, nodding.

"The last time I was at this house before you came, my sister was living here with your aunt. My sister didn't want to die in the hospital, so …"

"My aunt let her stay here, under her care." That was so Aunt Del: opening her home up to a terminal patient. Loving and caring for someone in their last moments.

"Mandy loved this view. The bog, and with the ocean in the background, way off in the distance."

"And that's why you're building your house."

He ran his hand through his hair. "Not my house; her house."

I threw my arms around him. "Let's go somewhere else. Somewhere without sad memories for you."

"I should be the one ending things, instead, I'm like this magnet drawn to you. I should be over … things … before I start a new relationship. It's not fair to drag you into my sadness—things shouldn't start like this."

"Look, we're both grieving. Maybe that makes us perfect to help each other. Maybe we can heal, a little bit, together. Because we don't have to pretend to be okay. We can just be. Together. Life is messy. There's good with the bad. You know? And this feels very good." I bumped him with my hip. Electricity coursed through me.

He looked at me, his expression concerned. And I had a doubt, deep in my core. We didn't really know each other. I was basically repeating my one-night stand move. Wanting someone to help me get over whatever I was feeling at the moment. It wasn't fair to Jesse. I should just put a stop to this. Now. Before it went any further. I took a breath to warn him. To tell him not to get involved with me. "Or maybe we shouldn't …"

"No. I'm not letting you push me away again." He ran his hand over his eyes and when he turned back to me, he was smiling impishly. "You feel *very* good. Let's make new memories here. Then I'll have both—the sad and—the not sad."

"Jesse …"

Before I could formulate an argument against what was happening, he lifted me by the waist and seated me up on the railing. His hands strong and sure. His touch; intoxicating. I was beyond reason. All I wanted was him. To feel him deep inside me, to chase away the well of grief there.

I opened my legs so he fit in between them and he kissed me hard. I leaned into him, feeling the thrill of only his strong grip keeping me from falling backward off the deck railing. I wrapped my hands around his neck and my fingers reached into his hair. Soft and silky, just as I had imagined.

He pressed harder, and I dangled out over nothingness, yet I had never felt safer—his arms enveloping me. I wrapped my legs around his back and pushed into him, moaning into his mouth: the good kind of moan. His hands roamed over my back and down to lift up my shirt. There was nothing between my skin and his fingers and it felt even better than in my fantasies. He rubbed my back in circles and unhooked my bra, before pulling me off the railing and carrying me to the lounger.

I came up for air long enough to ask if he wanted to go inside. He shook his head and his eyes were dark with passion. He sat down on the lounger, with me on top of him, and I unclasped my legs, pushing even harder into him, using the ground as leverage. He ran his hands down my back, over my butt, and down my legs, slipping my shoes off. I could feel him harden underneath me and all I could think of was him inside of me.

So, I whispered it. "Come inside me."

His hands were immediately at my head, pulling me back to his mouth, where his tongue swirled and pushed in mine. I moaned again. He grabbed my ass and flipped us over in one motion until I was lying on the lounge chair and he was straddling over me, his body no longer touching mine. I leaned into him to remedy that, but he slipped my shirt and bra over my head instead of joining our bodies together. He grabbed his shirt and pulled it off too as I ran my hands down his rippling muscles. He shivered in response, kissing my neck, standing above me, running his hands down to my waist. He pushed me back onto the lounger, unbuttoning my jeans, unzipping them and taking his time, pulling them slowly off my body.

"Please." This was taking so long; my skin buzzed from the want.

There was something amazing about my naked skin being kissed by him and the wind. By the touch of his fingers and the sun on my chest. By being outside and exposed to the elements of the island. By being exposed to him. I wanted more.

I wiggled out of my underwear and he backed up a step to look at me.

"Baby, come here," I demanded. Although lying there, exposed, not even being touched by anything except his look felt sweeter than I could have ever imagined. Like we were the only two people and had all the time in the world. Until my need for his touch grew too intense.

He smiled and closed his eyes like he was preserving the memory as a snapshot in his mind. I wiggled, needing his skin on my skin.

"You're so beautiful." In one step he closed the gap between us. He ran his fingers up my inner legs, to my thighs, parting my legs as he went. He eased the back of the lounger down, so I was lying flat, and kissed the trails his hands had left on my thighs. I shut my eyes and just *felt*. His lips and tongue moved slowly up my thighs until his fingers parted my sensitive skin down there and his lips found my clit.

His tongue darted inside me and I moaned—it was almost too

much. My hands found his head and I massaged his temple, matching the rhythm of his tongue.

"Baby come, for me." His breath tickled me and his tongue plunged back inside.

I couldn't answer, I was focusing on feeling everything his tongue was doing. His tongue left me and his mouth sucked on my clit and I moaned louder, and then he slipped his fingers inside me. Sucking and sliding. Until I couldn't take it any longer. I pulled his mouth up to mine and tasted him and me and felt his fingers massaging the inside of me until I let go into the muscle spasms around his fingers.

"Oh my god." He wasn't even naked. I relaxed into the warmth of the orgasm and my hands found his bulge in his jeans. I rubbed until he moaned and then undid his pants while he was still kneeling between my legs. He pulled a condom from his pocket and then stood to let his pants drop and pushed out of his underwear. I gazed at him, standing in the sunshine, naked and huge. He swiftly rolled the condom into place.

"Come inside me," I repeated, and it was more of a pleading than a demand. I could feel my body resetting and responding to him, again.

He pulled me up off the lounge and set me on his feet, holding me to him. We swayed a moment in the breeze to our own private song. His skin on my skin, the sun on my back. My fingers explored; first his back, then his taught butt, then one held onto his back while the other circled to the front. I wrapped my hand around him and rhythmically massaged him. I was wet all over again, just from touching him.

We swayed until it just got to be too much, and he sat down on the lounge chair, me over top of him, and in the same motion, he was inside me. Deep inside. My legs straddled the sides of the chair, pulling me even wider open, pulling him further inside. We both moaned together, and he arched up as he plunged deeper, wrapping his arms around so his hands held my butt cheeks. He arched, again and again, pulling me to him at the same time, plunging deeper and deeper until I couldn't take any more and cried out in release. One more plunge and he released too.

He pulled us to the side so we were lying on the lounger face to face, and he pushed some hair out of my eyes. "Mmm, baby, thanks for the new memory."

Every inch of my skin was sun kissed and Jesse-kissed, inside and out.

"You're welcome," I answered, closing my eyes and leaning my head to his chest.

For the first time in a while, I wasn't thinking about lists or to-dos or what would happen next.

I snuggled into Jesse, felt the sun and wind and his body on mine and gave in to the moment.

10

At some point during the night, Jesse carried me, more than half-asleep, up to my aunt's bedroom. He set me down gently and then crawled under the covers with me. I ran my hands over his naked skin and couldn't help but get aroused again. The room was completely black and I took advantage of the darkness.

This time, I explored every inch of him, slowly. With my fingertips, my palms, and my tongue. He ran his hands over my body as I moved down his body. I lifted my head up and told him, "That first night, I imagined your hands on my body when I showered and you stood outside the door."

"You were thinking of this? I was thinking I'd have to break down the door and make you come to the hospital. I thought maybe you had passed out in the shower." His voice was velvet in the dark.

"If you had broken down the door, we might have gotten here even sooner." I slid my hand my hands to cup his ass.

"I think we got here in the right amount of time. I wouldn't want us to start something because I rescued you."

Instead, we were starting something because I decided to use him to get over my grief. Heat rushed to my cheeks. I should say something. Explain it. Explain me. Explain that this wasn't the start of anything. But before I could, he spoke.

"I feel so untethered. Losing my sister. I mean, I didn't even know that we were so close growing up. She was always there. Like the witness to my life. Not pushing, not pulling, just letting me be who I am, even when I was a dumb kid."

I couldn't imagine him as a dumb kid. He seemed so confident. So self-assured.

"And now there's no one who knows me like that. I have friends, I have my parents, but you know, siblings are different. At least we were. I didn't honestly realize how close we were until she …" His voice trailed out into the dark room.

I shivered, thinking again about Mick. What would I do if Mick was gone? I took a shaky breath, and said, "I'm so sorry."

He shook his head and I felt the moment evaporating. And despite my decision earlier to make this just about getting through our grief, or honestly, maybe because of that, I dug my heals into the moment.

"Tell me about her. What was she like?"

"She was a pain in my ass." He rolled over and onto one elbow. The clouds parted outside the window and the moon threw light onto his grin.

"Hey, you don't have to do that." I rubbed his neck and saw that pain reappear.

"Do what?" he asked, even though I was pretty sure he knew.

"You don't have to make it seem like you're not in pain."

"We're both in pain." He turned away from me.

Maybe eyes on his pain were too much. I knew I felt that way most of the time. The moon went behind a cloud and we were plunged back into darkness. I got out of bed on my side, trailed around the bed, and slipped back in, facing away from him, but pushing my body against his. He pulled me in tight, folding me into his embrace.

"We *are* both in pain." I repeated his words.

And it was enough. He held me tighter and his words tripped

over themselves, like the lightning following the thunder the first night I slept here.

"I don't know who I am anymore. I've lost the person who knew my past, completely, the one I told everything to, and I've lost my future. Everything I was working on I was doing for Mandy. I moved to this island because it was her dream. I'm building a house for her. I put everything in my life on hold to get her as close to her dreams as possible. Because I knew. I knew. She didn't have a lot of time. And then she didn't."

He held on tight to me. Like he was a seatbelt, and we were heading for a crash. I didn't know what to say and didn't want to break the spell. Tears leaked out of my eyes, and I just let them roll down onto the pillow. I didn't know if I was crying for him, for his sister, for me, for my aunt, or for everyone.

"What do you do when you're living your life for someone else and then they leave?"

I didn't have an answer for that. I didn't have any answers. And the reality was that I could just leave this island and some of the pain over my aunt behind. I didn't have to live with the sadness every moment of every day. I could push it aside and go on with my life. And right now, that was exactly what I wanted to do. I had been naïve to think I could help someone through their grief; all I wanted was to sort through my aunt's belongings and put this whole island behind me. It was all too much. I was a coward. Jesse couldn't escape his grief, and here I was imagining myself on the ferry, with the island disappearing behind me. Leaving him and his pain behind.

"Hey, hey, hey." He moved one arm from around me to rub my arm. "Are you okay?"

I had thought I was hiding how uncomfortable I was, but I realized he could feel how tense my body had gotten.

I pushed out of his embrace and flipped over. "Stop it. Stop trying to take care of me—of everyone else. Don't ask me if I'm okay, when I should be taking care of you. Trying to help you with your pain. Don't let me off the hook." I could barely see him in the darkness, and that was probably a good thing. "I should be asking you if you are okay, and instead, I'm imagining leaving this island and my—everything—behind." Damn. I had meant to hide that. The cowardly part of myself that showed how truly awful I was. I turned away from him. *Great job, Paige, making it all about you.*

I lay still, not moving a muscle. "You should go. I'm a horrible person."

The bed shook, and I knew he was crying. Which made the sound I heard super confusing. Laughter. Like, a lot of laughter. Uncontrollable laughter.

I turned back toward him, and enough light filtered through the clouds that I could confirm, he was laughing. At me. What?

He touched my forehead; at the place I knew crinkled up when I was trying to figure something out. But his fingers shook with his laughter.

"You think you're a horrible person for wanting to escape when things get too heavy? I want to escape this island every single day." He got serious again and brushed the tears off my cheeks.

"No, I'm a horrible person to make your grief all about me!"

He pulled me into him and even though we were still both naked, that wasn't what was making me feel the most vulnerable, right at the moment.

"I've been grieving for a year now. And I'm tired of it. I don't have any answers after all this time, and I promised myself I wouldn't make your grief for your aunt all about my grief for my sister. And look what I did! Talk about self-absorbed."

"So, I'm a horrible person for making your grief all about me, and you're a horrible person to for making my grief all about you?"

"That's about how I'm seeing it right now. Although I don't think you're a horrible person. I just triggered your grief with my own. What I promised myself I wouldn't do."

"Oh, so you're a more horrible person than I am?" I couldn't help but giggle.

"For sure. One hundred percent."

"Oh, let's ask the Magic Eight Ball!"

"Of course, you have a Magic Eight Ball."

I switched on the bedside lamp and grabbed my keychain in my hand. Sat up, unconcerned with my lack of pajamas. "Magic Eight Ball, give us your wisdom!" I added a flourish to my normally no-nonsense Eight Ball routine. "Am I more of a horrible person than Jesse?" I shook it hard, jangling the keys as well.

YOU MAY RELY ON IT.

I showed Jesse the response and fell back into the pillows, laughing. "See!"

"Give me that thing." Jesse pulled it from my hands. "Could Paige ever be as horrible as I currently am?" He shook it like he was rolling dice at a craps table, and even held it out to me so I could blow on it.

MY SOURCES SAY NO.

"Well, there you have it. We're both self-absorbed, horrible people." Jesse pulled me back against his body. "At least now I don't have to be self-absorbed, horrible, and sad all by myself."

"I'll be self-absorbed, horrible, and sad with you." I turned around and took him into my arms.

"And want to run for the ferry every day?"

"And want to run for the ferry *every* day."

I didn't really know what had happened, but somehow, I felt better than I had since I had gotten the word about my aunt.

"How's your head?" He massaged my scalp. Gently around where the bump was.

"I totally forgot about it."

"Let's hope you start forgetting about the other pain in your life."

"Hey, that wasn't horrible or self-absorbed." I snuggled deeper into him and he shifted so he was now holding me.

"I'll try to be more horrible and self-absorbed tomorrow." His voice drifted like he was on the verge of sleep.

"That's my man."

"I'm your man?"

"Until I can find someone even more horrible and self-absorbed."

"Hey." His voice was firm.

I opened my eyes.

"We can joke about grief making us bad for the rest of the world, but don't even joke about finding someone like that. I got a good look at your ex today, and I did NOT like what I saw. He's dangerous." Jesse gently held my head in his hands. "Promise me you're done with him."

I was too tired to get into it with him. "You sound like Matt." My heavy eyelids slid low and I wished Jesse would just let me go to sleep.

"Matt sounds very smart." The bed shifted as Jesse sat up. "Promise me."

I opened one eye. "I was already done with him."

"Sure?" He reached behind me and clicked off the light.

"It is decidedly so."

"You truly are horrible." Jesse tucked me into his body like he was protecting me from the world, and maybe even, myself.

I sighed happily and let the distant sound of waves lull me to sleep.

★★★

Jesse was sleeping peacefully when I woke, wanting coffee more than I'd ever wanted anything before, except maybe him. The night had been extraordinary and the fact that he was still in my bed—available to me, to do more, experience it again, was unbelievable.

The coffee dripping in the machine, I tiptoed back upstairs to jump in the shower. Then back down to collect coffee mugs and make us both a cup. I filled a tray with mugs of coffee and snacks and milk and sugar. By the time I got back upstairs, he was walking out of the bathroom with a towel around his waist. I hadn't even heard the shower going.

"It's beautiful outside—let's take this onto the back deck," I suggested, happy that he was awake. We got dressed, passing each other in the bedroom and bathroom, me handing him an extra toothbrush my aunt always kept on hand for surprise visitors and him touching me somewhere every time we got close.

On the deck, we sat together, enjoying the silence, the coffee, and the sunny morning.

I could get used to this. And as idyllic as it was, it didn't feel like vacation. It felt like life. Real-life. I answered a couple of panic texts from Sheila to calm her down. He delayed going to work for an hour and we talked about what was left to do for the celebration. When Margo's brother, Drew, showed up with a couple of boxes of wine, we finally got to work.

It was fun, the two of us stringing lights over the deck and over the backyard. Setting up tables—long ones for showcasing my aunt's items for people to take, small ones for people to gather around and set their drinks and food. Placing chairs in groups around the non-sloped parts of the backyard.

When Bells showed up, Jesse got up to leave for work. I walked him to his truck.

"I know we didn't talk about Frank all that much today—if he comes by, text me; I'll be right over."

"He's just sad. His mom died and he feels lost—I was a part of his family, you know. I'm sure he took a ferry off the island this morning. I made it clear, I don't want to get back together, but I'm here for him." I didn't know why I kept defending Frank.

It looked like he was fighting testosterone. "Just call me if he shows up—I'll be right over. Promise me."

I nodded. We shared a lingering kiss until Bells knocked into us, carrying supplies toward the house.

"Okay, you love birds, if we are going to hold an island-wide party to commemorate Delilah tomorrow, we're going to not spend our time with our tongues down each other's throats."

"Bells ..."

"She's used to getting her way, and I think she could take the both of us, so we should definitely obey." Jesse strode over to his truck, got in, and waved goodbye.

"Well, you look like the cat that swallowed the canary. I'm glad you guys finally got together." Bells tipped the box toward me so I could see the contents. Flameless candles.

"Finally? I've only been here a few days!" I pulled some candles from her box.

"Well, you know what Einstein said about time, right? That 'the distinction between past, present, and future is only a stubbornly persistent illusion.'"

"Wait, what does that mean?" I ran after Bells as she strode into the house. I knew I was on leave from work, and planning a memorial for my aunt, but could life get any better than this? I showed Bells my Magic Eight Ball keychain and let her shake it, asking it that question: Did life get any better than this? CONCENTRATE AND ASK AGAIN.

But I didn't need to—I knew this was the best I'd felt, the most "me" I'd felt in forever. I knew that the friends I made on the island were so kind and immediate because we had my aunt in common. Because we all loved her. But the friendship felt so true. Grief was a funny thing. I felt sad and loved at the same time. Happy and empty. Empowered and Lost. Feeling all the things that made me know I was truly living.

Thank you, Aunt Del, for everything.

11

Bells lined up all the boxes of things that would go out tomorrow and be placed on the tables. On top, she carefully put the big doilies and tablecloths and baskets to arrange things nicely. Annoying, she told me that her Einstein quote meant whatever I wanted it to mean.

"Don't you have to work today?" I folded a tablecloth and placed it on the last box.

"Not until lunchtime. I want to make sure that we're all set up." She gestured to the cluttered chaos around us.

I started cleaning up the house—vacuuming and wiping things down. I was still thinking about all the things, all at once. Mindless cleaning allowed my thoughts to wander. I was feeling more in tune with Einstein when I thought back to my words to Jesse yesterday—that life was messy and maybe if we found something good, we should grab it even though we were both dealing with, well, life. Bells came running in from the shed, where she had been cleaning up. "Hey, your aunt's here, and that's perfect because I have to get to work."

"What?" For one second, my heart skipped a beat. Like, maybe my Aunt Del wasn't really gone, and this had all been a big mistake.

And then I realized. It must be my Aunt Sally. What was she doing here? I ran out to meet her, with Bells in tow.

"Hey, honey." She swooped in and gave me a big hug. "I got the email invite for the party and came early to see if you needed any help."

"What email invite?" I hugged her hard. Images of her and my mom and aunt flooded my mind.

Bells shrugged. "We sent an email to the whole island, and I guess, anyone who signed up for updates from the cultural center. You know, the whole mailing list. We wanted to make sure that anyone who knew your aunt would get the memo."

"Oh, that's ... nice." My stomach knotted up. I let go of my aunt. This no longer felt like a fun impromptu outdoor party—it was starting to feel like a Big Deal. As it should—everyone who knew my aunt should be invited. Aunt Delilah deserved a big deal. I swallowed. "Thank you, Bells, that was totally the right call."

"Where should I put my bags?"

This seemed like a weird question—since, with the arrival of my aunt, it felt like I was no longer in charge. In fact, it felt a little as if I was a kid again. I was going to have to get over that quickly. I wasn't a kid. And I was in charge.

"Um, I'm in Aunt Del's bedroom, so I guess the upstairs guest room?"

"Honey, thanks for doing this for Del. I was crushed I couldn't go to her memorial. Crushed."

"Wait, why couldn't you?" Maybe I'd get some insight to why Aunt Sally disappeared from the photo album during my mom's illness.

My aunt wiggled her fingers at me as she dragged her Louis Vuitton suitcase over the gravel and up the stairs to the house. "That is a story for another time, or maybe never. Life's too short, you know?"

I looked at Bells as if she might know the answer. Maybe she could pull out another Einstein quote. She shrugged. "Families."

"Right." I waved her goodbye and thanked her for all the help. There was so much work still to do now that I knew that the whole world was coming to my aunt's house tomorrow. And even with her perfectly manicured nails, I knew Aunt Sally would work as hard as anyone. I shot off a text to Jesse to keep him informed.

I was right: My aunt made quick work of the cleanup. Her red hair flying, she buzzed around the house with a force that reminded me of the storm from my first night on the island. The house was back to its usual, neat self, albeit a little empty, by dinner. We had amassed a final pile of trash bags that were stored neatly in the shed, and all the items that would be placed outside had nice neat hand-calligraphed labels, all ready to be set out in the morning.

Jesse stopped by to pick us up for a picnic dinner near the southern lighthouse, which appeared to be closed for renovations, and to watch the ferries come in and go out.

My aunt shared stories of Aunt Del that I had never heard before. Jesse's grin widened as each story got more outlandish. I could tell he was loving my aunt. My phone buzzed and I looked down. My mom texted:

Surprise, honey, I'm here!
Here? Where?
Ferry Dock. Come get me?

I sat staring at my phone long enough that it was rude. And then a bit longer. And longer.

"Babe?"

I looked up. How to explain all this weird family drama that was suddenly in our laps? I put my wine glass down on the cooler's top.

And then another text came in.

I need you. – from Frank.

"Aunt Sally?"

My aunt was gazing out at the sky darkening over the water. "Yes, my dear?"

"Um ..."

My phone buzzed again.

There seem to be no taxis here—help! – my Mom

Pls Call — from Frank

Hold on. I texted this twice and looked up. Jesse was waiting patiently for me to explain. My aunt was still staring out at the sea.

"Um, so I think Mom is here."

"Here, here? Why didn't you tell me she was coming? Why is she coming? Is it not enough that I don't get to attend the funeral of my own sister, but now she has to take over this memorial too?" My aunt stood in a cyclone of movement, packing up our picnic dinner so quickly I was sure some random sand creatures got swept up and thrown into the bag.

"Um, so my mom…" I tried to explain to Jesse something I didn't really understand.

"Is stuck in the past."

"… And my aunt …"

"Can't do anything right."

"So, my mom needs a ride." I looked down at the ferry dock, within view, but so far away. I couldn't see my mom, but I knew she was there, somewhere.

"Don't worry about me, I'll walk back to the house."

"Don't be—"

"Ridiculous? It's not me who's ridiculous."

"It's a long, and soon to be, dark, walk to Del's. Why don't you just sit up front in the cab and Paige and her mom can sit in the back?" Jesse stood up and grabbed the picnic bag.

I gave Jesse what I hoped was a look that said, thank-you-for-trying-to-smooth-over-this-insanity. Then I climbed into the backseat, steeled for the most uncomfortable ten minutes of my life, while I tried to reorganize everything I thought about my family.

It's all going to be okay. It's all going to be okay.

But was it? My aunt had really flipped that my mom was here. In pictures in the family photo albums when the three sisters were young, they had all seemed so close and happy—which was contrary to my thoughts growing up that my mom and her sister just didn't like one another. I hadn't questioned it; it was simply my family's dynamic. But my aunt seemed so angry that she hadn't been allowed at Aunt Del's funeral, and I hadn't even known that. I thought it was her who couldn't attend for some reason. I didn't get far into my musings before Jesse parked the truck in the ferry parking lot.

I jogged down the ferry pier to my mom, who was dragging her suitcase behind her. Short, thin, and spunky, with her brown hair pulled back in a ponytail. I hugged her tight, grabbed her suitcase, and ignored her chatter about all the things she wanted to bake before the start of the party. I couldn't get a word in edgewise and wasn't really sure what I'd say if I could.

Baking was her new thing since she had retired, and she was really great at some of the basic stuff she'd been baking all our lives, but recently she'd started mixing weird things together. Her concoctions never really worked. Some were downright disgusting. Bacon and chocolate. Jalapeno and berries. Things that chefs around the world were doing, but my mom was not a professional chef, and *really* not great at the weird combos. Her words flew in one ear and out the other.

I didn't tell her that the desserts were being provided by Penny at the cafe, or that her arch-nemesis, her own sister, was not only in town, but currently inside the only transportation we had.

As we approached the truck, I was happy to see Jesse leaning nonchalantly at the driver's side door. *It's all going to be okay. It's all going to be okay.*

Maybe I should give her the head's up. Or maybe she should have been more honest with me about why we never saw Aunt Sally. What I knew about my family was shifting in front of my eyes and I didn't even know what to say.

"Mom, this is Jesse. He's been amazing while I've been on the island."

"Hi Jesse, I'm Greta. It's so nice to meet you!" She raised her eyebrows and smiled at me. Jesse grabbed the suitcase and put it in the truck bed.

"Um, mom, don't freak out, but ..."

"You're dating Jesse? That happened fast." My mom's smile turned into a wide grin.

"Yes, it happened fast. But also, Aunt Sally is here too." I pointed to the cab while I steered my mom to the backseat.

"What? Why?" My mom's face turned a bright shade of pink.

"She just decided to come. And since the house is now mine, you are both invited and welcome."

"I'll just ..."

"Mom, get in; we'll figure everything else out later." I ushered her up into the truck and closed the door behind her.

"Hey, do you want to tell me why they don't get along?" Jesse caught me by the waist as I rounded the truck.

"That's just it, I don't actually know." I hugged him and wondered whether we could ignore the family stuff. I mean, we were just starting a new relationship, getting to know each other. We were already working through grief together. Adding a mysterious family drama into the mix couldn't be wise.

My mom's door popped open again. She gingerly climbed out of the truck. "Give me my suitcase, I'll find lodging at a hotel."

"Mom. Get into the car." I pointed to the back seat.

"I didn't know Sally was coming." She scanned the strip of shops and her eyes settled on the Grand Hotel at the end of the street.

"I didn't either." I shook my head.

"You didn't tell me she was here." She put her hands on her hips.

"You didn't tell me you were coming. If you had given me the head's up ..." I shook my head. I had no idea what the end of that sentence should be.

Bu there was also nothing she could say to that. She held out her hand, presumably for her suitcase. Jesse looked at me. I shook my head, again.

"Let's sort this out at Aunt Del's house, not in the middle of the parking lot, Mom."

She stood and deliberated for a moment and then it seemed like decorum won. She climbed back into the truck. I quickly headed for my side so she wouldn't have time to change her mind again.

Jesse got in and started the engine, and there was an uncomfortable silence for a moment. Then he chatted about all the things we passed and the sights to see on the island. Neither my aunt Sally nor my mom said a word. Neither were generally quiet people, so I grew more and more anxious as the drive progressed. If I had thought the drive to the pier in anticipation of my mom's arrival was awkward, this one was a hundred times worse. I also decided I no longer wanted to know why my aunt and mom didn't get along. They were adults—they could sort it out on their own. This week wasn't about them.

My cell dinged: **How long should I hold on?** – from Frank. Oh, I had forgotten about him.

I'll call you in a few.

We arrived at Aunt Del's house, finally. Aunt Sally grabbed the picnic bag and stomped into the house. I didn't even know if she had acknowledged my mom at all. Jesse walked my mom's suitcase in and placed it in the downstairs guest room at my suggestion. I could hear Sally bumping around upstairs in her room.

"Well, this is stunning! Look at the beautiful sunset!" My mom held out her arms like she was embracing the whole island. It was like a light switch had turned on once my aunt was out of sight.

"It's the same sunset as it was when we were driving over, and you sat and sulked. But once I'm gone, it's beautiful?" My aunt thundered down the stairs, yelling.

"There's no reason to make a scene, Sally."

My phone started ringing. Why on earth had I un-blocked Frank's number? I sent him a text instead of answering the call: **Family drama. Call you in a bit.**

"Why don't we have a glass of wine out on the deck?"

"I'm going to call it a day." Aunt Sally wiggled her fingers at me. "Bye, Paige, dear; bye, Jesse. Thanks for the picnic!"

And then she was gone, back up the stairs.

"Mom, maybe you and Sally could just ..."

"You're just like Del. Always trying to fix things. Just let it be, Paige Elliot."

She used her stern mom voice which told me the conversation was over before it began. And she used my middle name: double over. My mom rifled through the picnic bag I hadn't yet unpacked and grabbed a bottle of wine. "Wine sounds perfect, but I will take it in my room. See you both in the morning." She grabbed a bottle opener, and walked out of the room. I exchanged a look with Jesse, who was still with us, through all the family weirdness.

"You okay?" He put his hand on my back and rubbed.

The touch immediately melted some of my stress. Reminded me of how good things were when we were alone. I could use a stress relief right about now. I leaned into him. I imagined my mom in the cheery yellow guest room, head thrown back, guzzling directly from the wine bottle.

"I guess? Not much to do—I don't know why they have never gotten along." But that photo album told a different story—the story of three close sisters.

Jesse's phone buzzed. He took a quick look. "Damn. I'm so sorry. I'm the one on call for emergency support and need to go." He pulled me all the way into his arms. "If it wasn't literally an emergency, I wouldn't leave you right now. I'll be back in the morning to help you set up for the party, though. Okay?"

Things had changed so quickly—like a cyclone. My aunt and my mom heading their separate ways, and now Jesse. My phone buzzed too. I knew who it was without looking. "That's totally okay. I should try to get some sleep." And talk to my ex.

"Hey. I don't want to go. You know that, right?"

I sighed. "Of course. My mom and aunt coming just threw me for a loop."

He kissed the top of my head and held me until his phone vibrated between us.

I pulled back. "I'll be fine. Really. Go."

"Call me for *anything*. I mean it." He reluctantly released me.

I watched him walk to his car in the gathering dusk and called out, "Thank you so much for the wonderful day!" I didn't want him going without knowing how grateful I was that he took all my family's weirdness in stride.

I thought my mom might have the right idea and grabbed a bottle of wine from the cabinet. Thank goodness Margo was donating wine for the party—I was almost all the way through all my aunt's stash. I took it upstairs and poured a large glass before clicking on one of Frank's missed calls from my phone's call list.

"Paige?" He slurred the 'g' in my name as if it was a very long 'sh.'

"Frank. Sorry I couldn't call earlier; it's been crazy. How are you?"

"I'm missing my girlfriend. Come to the bar." I heard voices in the background—voices I thought I actually recognized.

"You're still on the island?!"

"Of course, I am. I couldn't leave without my Paigggge."

There was so much to unpack there; I didn't even know where to begin. And not that it would help. There was no sense in reasoning with a very drunk Frank. I settled back into bed, ready to listen to whatever rant he wanted to start next. By my second glass of wine, I found I could just murmur agreement and he kept talking. I plugged in my phone and put it on speaker mode and laid my head down on the pillow. I'd just rest my eyes for a moment while he talked.

★★★

There was a loud knock downstairs on the front door and Bells' cheery voice yelled out, "Hello! Who's ready for a window install?"

I groggily opened my eyes. Bright sunlight streamed through the window and puddled on the middle of the bed. I sat up and tried to clear my throat so it didn't sound like I was just waking up, which of course, I was. "Bells, c'mon in. I'll be right down!"

Was today going to be less chaotic than yesterday? I shook my keychain. BETTER NOT TELL YOU NOW. Damn, Eight Ball. Couldn't you give a girl some hope?

I quickly brushed my teeth and put on new jeans and a blouse and threw my hair in a ponytail. Hoping my phone hadn't run out of battery while I fell asleep listening to Frank last night. Nope, thank you, tech gods, for reminding me to plug it in last night. Frank still being on the island was a problem for later.

I took the stairs two at a time and careened into the kitchen. Thankfully, Bells held two coffees in her hands, and handed me one while the brightness of the day streamed through the intact kitchen windows and smacked me square on the face.

My mom waved to me from the deck where she sat, book in hand in the sunlight. Even more thankfully, Jesse stood there, looking tired but happy to see me. He pulled me into a hug and guided me through the house and out to the driveway, where his truck sat in front of Xavier's.

Xavier stood at the back of his pickup, expertly releasing the bungee cords holding a giant bay window encased in a wood box from the bed.

"Paige, Xavier. Xavier, Paige."

"We've met. Xavier hauled some stuff to the recycling center for me." I waved hello, and Xavier nodded back. He seemed slightly less gruff than he was before. His baseball cap hung low over his eyes, so I couldn't really see their expression, but his mouth was no longer in a stern line.

"Xav, I might need a hand at the house in a few days, if you have some time." Jesse and Xavier continued talking as they unloaded the new window. Bells grabbed a corner, so I did too. It was huge and heavy.

"Sure. Has Paige seen the house yet?"

Wow. Xavier was definitely in a better mood.

We shuffle-stepped the window up the porch and around the house, slowly making our way to the back.

"Not yet. There's still not much to see. That last batch of monkey bread was so good—tell your mom." Jesse wasn't out of breath at all.

"Everything I've eaten of Penny's is like the best thing I've ever eaten. And then the next thing is even better." I huffed out the words.

"My mom loves to hear that. I'll tell her you said so." Xavier's tone was very soft, and I wondered what had made him so grumpy the last time we met.

"Thanks. Your mom ... awesome baker ... love her ... everything." I knew I sounded like an idiot, but trying to speak and keep the window from crashing to the deck was all I could muster.

We shuffled around the corner and into the homestretch. My fingers and arms ached and all I could think about was putting the huge window down. I wanted to yell, Could we please put it down?! Or better yet, just drop it. But I swallowed my wimpy thoughts. For everyone else, including Bells, carrying this heavy thing seemed like a walk in the park.

"Yeah, she's pretty great at cooking." Xavier shrugged. I couldn't help admire his muscles rippling underneath the back of his shirt and wish that I was on the same side of the window as Jesse, so I could focus on *his* physique, instead of his friend's.

My mom sat at the glass table on the deck, reading a book. She stood up as we got close. "Do you need a hand?"

Oh, my god, yes, Mom, we needed a hand. Instead of saying that, I focused on the last few steps and on just holding the damn thing steady.

"We're good, thanks, Greta." Jesse didn't sound like he was holding a feather, let alone a bay window. I channeled the confidence from Jesse's voice and tried to hold on. Just a few steps more. I could totally do it. Maybe.

"Mom, this is Bells and Xavier." I squeaked the words out. I was going to have to start lifting weights to keep up with this crowd.

We maneuvered the window until it was leaning against the house. Finally, I released it. I sank to the deck and exhaled hard.

"Anyone like a snack?" Even at my aunt's house, which was now really my house, my mom was a considerate hostess.

"Definitely, in a few minutes, once we get this installed!" Bells ran to my mom. "So nice to meet you!"

Bells and my mom were going to get along just fine; instead of a handshake, they both went in for the hug.

Xavier left quickly for another job, saying he'd be back that night to celebrate my aunt. My mom and I settled into the deck chairs sipping coffee, turned to watch the window installation, rather than the scenic bog. Bells and Jesse made quick work of taking the plywood off the house and installing the new window, pulling out tool after tool from a tool bag slung over Jesse's shoulder.

I sipped the coffee, watching Jesse's confident movements.

"I'm sorry I made a scene with your aunt. I was just taken by surprise."

I decided to not weigh in on something my mom didn't think I should be privy to. I said nothing. Maybe it was passive-aggressive, or maybe it was just not trying to air my family's weirdness in front of people.

"Your aunt left early this morning for a bike ride, thank goodness, before I woke up. She left a note saying she'd be back later." At some point, my mom had swapped coffee for wine. She took a big sip. "Let's order pizza."

"Pizza would be perfect!" Bells grabbed a glass of wine and settled in. "Tell me stories of little Paige."

I shook my head and rolled my eyes. The best way for my new friends to get to know me wasn't exactly hearing childhood tales from my mom.

"I have a few errands to run. I can pick up the pizza on the way back. And, I know you just got here, Greta, but would it be okay to steal Paige for the errands?" Jesse pulled me into his side.

Bells waved her wine glass, answering instead of my mom. "Take your time. Greta and I are going to get to know one another."

"Go ahead, honey, I'll be more than fine." My mom leaned conspiratorially across the table toward Bells.

I sighed and took my empty coffee cup inside, Jesse at my heels. Once the slider was closed, he asked, "Is this okay? I thought you might need a break from the family. Can I be that break?"

Impulsively, I grabbed his face in my hands and kissed him firmly on the lips, leaning in and opening up to his tongue. When we parted finally, I pleaded, "Please, take me away."

12

I grabbed his hand like a teenager, and we ran from the house like someone was going to stop us and pull us back into family drama. Or, at least I felt that way. I wanted to leave quickly before my aunt showed up again and started a fight with my mom.

Finally, safely in the truck, I asked, "What errands?"

"First, let's order the pizza. And then I want to show you my sister's house." He pulled out his phone and the longer we sat in the truck parked in the driveway, I worried that my mom would come out and ask us to come back in, or that my aunt would come back from her ride and engage us in some conversation. Jesse and I discussed pizza options, and we went with the local pizza place's specials: one veggie special, one meat special, as well as one plain cheese.

Then we escaped. Jesse drove us on winding roads around the coast of the island, pointing things out as we went. A second lighthouse on the northern tip. Cliffs. A jungle-like maze of walks. A beautiful pond in the interior of the island. Every moment it seemed that there was something else to see and do. Again, I had the thought: maybe I would keep my aunt's house to vacation in and rent it out when I wasn't on the island. Clearly, there was so much island I hadn't yet discovered. I could come on the weekends and spend time with Jesse.

Jesse's hand reached out to rub my back, massaging all the way up to my neck. With his eyes still on the road, he kneaded my muscles. "You're so tense. Your neck got stiff as soon as your mom texted you."

"She doesn't normally stress me out. We're really close. But you saw my mom and my aunt together—it's awful."

It was sweet that he had noticed that. That whole picnic had been sweet. Until my mom had texted. Frank too. Oh no. Frank. I pulled my phone from my purse and saw that he had texted and called A LOT this morning.

"And you just got tenser, if that is possible."

"Frank texted. And called. Like twenty times."

Jesse's muscled fingers dug into my neck in a way that hurt, but relaxed me after they moved on to the next knot. Releasing my tension circle after circle. His thumb pressed deeply into the side of my neck and I moaned. It hurt so much and then felt amazing.

"Don't answer that asshole. Just block him. I know you said he was going through something, but so are you. Focus on yourself." His hand slid down my back, and around to my thigh, where he kept circling my muscles with his fingers, swirling higher and higher up my thigh. Electricity shot through my body and I responded immediately.

"I just want to be here, with you, in this moment." I remembered the stranger on the ferry telling me I was going to miss out on the best things if I didn't focus on what was right in front of me. He was right. I chucked my phone into the side pocket of the truck. Everything else could wait.

I turned my body toward him, amazed at how quickly I went from stressed to eager. Focused only on him and the feelings he produced inside my body.

"We're here."

We were in a sandy lot, with trees circling us and thick foliage on all sides, except a wooden structure—the beginning of a house—straight ahead, peeking out between tall evergreen trees.

I leaned into him, wanting to explore the electricity firing through my body.

"Baby, let me show you what I'm building."

I got shivers whenever he called me "Baby." I wanted to hold onto that feeling and let it grow. And then pounce on him.

We followed the dirt path between the trees that opened into a spectacular view. The house was only a multi-level platform on a foundation, with two-by-fours framing the basic shape. I could see all the way through the house to views overlooking lush green bogs all the way out to the craggy shoreline and the ocean. "It's breathtaking."

He beamed like a kid winning a science fair project. "I've been working on it so long; piece by piece. Seeing it with you is like seeing it again for the first time." He took me on a tour, pointing out the frames for the bathrooms, the expansive main living space, and kitchen, both in the back of the house, overlooking the view. We walked up the staircase and suddenly it felt like we were in the clouds. I touched the frame. He was building this whole house with his hands. Creating something beautiful from nothing.

My anxiety from the actions of my mom, my aunt, and Frank dissipated.

"Words can't even, about this view." I sat down on the very edge of the platform that would become the second floor of the house, my feet dangling over the side. Looking over the lush green bog, the faraway houses, to the expansive ocean. And then because I was amazed at this man who could build something beautiful where there was nothing before, this man who seemed to be able to do anything, I said, "Tell me about your sister."

He didn't hesitate, but started talking while settling down next to me. "She was a bright light for me my whole life. And always so optimistic about her illness and living life to the fullest, that I never actually thought we'd lose her. Took me by surprise even with the doctors—and your aunt—trying to prepare me. I just didn't think she'd actually leave us."

Birds tweeted around us and waves crashed in the distance. "I wake up each morning thinking she's still with us and then I lose her all over again. It makes me not want to go to sleep at all."

Oh, my god. There wasn't anything I could say to that, so I just pulled him to me and held him as tightly as I could. He stiffened like he was going to push me away, and then relaxed into my arms. I thought of those pictures of my mom and her sisters looking so happy in their childhood and asked him about growing up with her.

He told me of their childhood on the mainland—of her on-again-off-again illness—and how they had a basically happy time as kids. How she dreamed of living on the island, so they moved on when they were both older. How their parents helped finance an apartment until they could swing it on their own. How they were close with aunts and uncles and cousins and had family reunions on the island.

"I mean, it wasn't all sunshine and rainbows. She infuriated me on a regular basis. But never for long. Living with her illness, we didn't have the luxury of staying angry at each other. And I guess, I convinced myself that she was going to live with that illness for a whole long life. I convinced myself she'd live in this house."

I hugged him tightly and slid down until his head rested on my shoulder and we lay staring at the natural ceiling of roaming clouds. His breathing slowed until I was pretty sure he was asleep. I watched the clouds float over the distant ocean and let the birds lull me into my own thoughts.

I thought of how often he had shown up at my aunt's house in the middle of the night. How he had seemed like he never slept, and I started to understand his state of mind and state of being.

It all started to feel very big. How was I supposed to help him heal?

I had lost my aunt, yes, and it definitely untethered me, but not in this same way. And I lived on the mainland. It was only an hour drive to the ferry and an hour ferry ride, but it seemed like he needed so much more right now. So much more than a part-time girlfriend. If that was even what I was. And this still felt like a vacation. Once I immersed myself back into work, could I even take off weekends to spend time with him? I normally worked all the time—I wanted to become a partner in the marketing company or learn enough to start my own business. How could I do all that and be what he needed right now?

His phone vibrated in his jeans pocket. Which sent my thoughts flying to Frank and all his unanswered texts and calls. Guilt crashed onto me. Guilt for not being there for Frank; guilt for allowing this to go this far with Jesse, knowing I couldn't very well be there for him. I untangled myself from Jesse, trying not to wake him, and stared at his muscular body for only a moment before I jogged back down the stairs and to the truck. I didn't want him to wake without me there, not after what he shared, but I also wanted to ease my guilt about Frank.

I grabbed my phone. It was littered with missed calls and texts. But nothing that seemed important. And as soon as I got out of sight of Jesse, all I wanted was to get back to him. Stressed that he would wake without me and think I didn't understand the weight of all the things he had just told me.

I was torn. Should I stay and call Frank back? No, I was more concerned about Jesse. About him waking up without me there after opening up to me. What would that feel like? Like I abandoned him?

I ran back to the second floor of the house. By the time I got back, Jesse was talking on the phone. "We'll be right over. Thanks for keeping it hot." Shoving the phone in his pocket, he turned to me. "Pizza's more than ready. Should we re-enter your family drama?"

Thankfully, he didn't seem too bothered by waking up alone. But I felt awful.

I looked down at my phone. Guilt continued to eat away at

how I was mishandling everything. It seemed like I couldn't be what anyone needed, let alone what everyone needed. I knew I should pull him into my arms, to hold him, but I couldn't get out from under the stress. My mom waiting for the pizza with Bells. Us leaving them together for too long, when they didn't know each other at all. My aunt possibly returning and starting things up with my mom. Frank needing more than I could offer. Suddenly everyone seemed to need more than I could humanly, physically, give.

My stomach growled.

"Let's get that pizza." I had to start somewhere, and food seemed about right, although at the moment, with everything seeming so big, I had a strong desire to have Jesse drop me off at the ferry and leave all this behind. Throw my phone into the ocean and forget everything that had happened over the last few weeks. I couldn't bring back Jesse's sister; I couldn't bring back Frank's mom. Couldn't bring back Aunt Del.

I had to be strong for Jesse, for what he was going through, but for some inexplicable reason, I felt that if he reached out and touched me, I would burst into tears. *Get it together, Paige. You have to be there for him.* But I didn't think I had the strength. I could barely be there for myself, let alone carry everyone else.

I turned from Jesse and walked down the stairs. Out of his unfinished house, wishing I could be back in my comfortable, orderly, predictable life.

I was a horrible person, and I didn't want to joke about it like we had the other night.

★★★

If Jesse was confused about how suddenly I couldn't bring myself to talk, he didn't let on. We grabbed the pizzas and headed back to the house.

Instead of walking through the front door of my aunt's house, I carried the pizza around the wrap-around porch.

Before I got to the corner of the back, Jesse nudged me with a wine bottle he had picked up with the pizza. "Hey, you okay?"

"Of course, why wouldn't I be?" I turned the corner and plastered a smile on my face for my mom's and Bells' benefit.

"I don't know. You just seem distant. Maybe I over-shared."

"Oh my gosh, no. I'm just thinking. There's a lot going on right now." I said it in a low tone like it was a secret. "Hi, Mom; hey, Bells," I almost yelled. What was wrong with me?

They were munching on snack food from Aunt Del's kitchen. I didn't know why I had been worried about staying away so long. They were clearly managing well on their own. And Aunt Sally was nowhere to be seen.

"We found your list of things to do before the party. I think we finished everything except hanging the lights back here. I didn't want to put your mom on the ladder." Bells giggled.

Oh my god. I looked up to the sky as if the party gods would show me how much time there was before people would arrive. My feelings of everything being too much and not having the answers grew in intensity, if that was at all possible. I could hardly breathe.

I put the pizza on the table. Bells and my mom had already brought out plates and wine glasses so I sat down. One thing at a time. One person at a time. One bite at a time. One sip of wine at a time. One string of lights at a time.

"Jesse, Bells, let's get those lights up." I tried to keep my voice level, like I wasn't feeling like I was about to hyperventilate.

"Slow down. You can finish a slice of pizza first, you know." Jesse's voice sounded confused and concerned. And why not? He had just opened up to me about the most painful time in his life, and I had left him to go get my phone from the car? Even I was confused about my actions.

I searched each face turned toward me. Bells, kind and eager; my mom, enjoying the moment; Jesse, concerned and supportive. "I guess I'm feeling anxious about the party—it would make me feel so much better if I knocked this last thing off my to-do list."

Bells stuffed the rest of her pizza in her mouth and yelled, "I'll get the ladder!"

Jesse studied me like he wanted to say something, ran his hand through his hair, and nodded. "Okay. Whatever you need."

Which I thought was a pretty weird comment at the moment. The lights were on my to-do list. The last thing. Of course, they needed to be hung. It wasn't just my need. It was the party's need. Not mine. I pushed the pizza plate away and headed down to the lawn.

For the first time, I took in the sight. Bar-height circular tables stood at intervals, prettily done up with white tablecloths and flowers. All kinds of flowers, different on each table. Some small violets, some azaleas, some big fuchsia flowers I couldn't name. All beautiful. Bigger arrangements of flowers in pots on long tables lining the deck, with baskets of collections of my aunt's things. A guest book open to a blank page, alongside the photo albums I had been looking at all week. Bells and her friends had outdone themselves. One table was filled with wine glasses and red wine bottles.

Bells hefted the ladder over to me. "Margo has the white wine bottles chilling in the fridge. We'll bring them down before the party. That table will be for the food." She pointed to the one table empty of anything except some flowers.

"It's so beautiful, Bells. Thank you."

"Wasn't just me. Everyone helped. We all miss Delilah."

And that's when it hit me. This wasn't about me at all. This whole week should have been about my aunt, and at some point, I made it about me. How selfish could I be? This was about Aunt Delilah and everyone who loved her. Not about why my mom and Sally couldn't get along. Not about whether or not I should start something up with a great guy when I was planning on going back to the mainland and my normal life. Not about my ex, who wanted me to comfort him through his own loss.

It was about celebrating my aunt and her amazing life. All the lives she touched. All the people she loved. It was time to stop being so selfish. Put Aunt Del at the center of all things.

Jesse pulled out strings of lights from a few boxes under the rectangular tables.

"This is perfect. My aunt would love this. We're going to have the best party." I hugged Jesse as soon as he stood upright. "Thank you." He held me one beat longer than a normal hug and seemed to resist letting me go.

We strung the bulbs, crisscrossing above the circular tables, and Jesse and Bells even pounded a stake in the ground when we needed another anchor point besides the sporadic trees. I turned on the lights immediately, and even though you couldn't see them yet in the daylight, my mom clapped from the deck.

Jesse gave me a quick kiss on the lips and smiled. "I'm going to go get ready, but I'll be back soon. Penny said she and Walter would come by a little early to arrange the food, and I think that's it, right? Nothing left on your to-do list?"

Was there anything else I could do to make Aunt Del's memorial a success? I took the tiny Magic Eight Ball keychain from my pocket. REPLY HAZY TRY AGAIN.

Yup, Magic Eight Ball, I felt that way too. We had accomplished everything that was in our control, but would my family behave long enough to honor my aunt?

I shrugged at Jesse, anxiety mounting again. He gave me a sheepish grin and I frowned at the dark circles under his eyes. I didn't feel like I was enough to keep this party on its tracks, Frank in his place, or most importantly, Jesse healing from his loss.

And if Aunt Del's funeral had been any indicator, everything that could go wrong, probably would.

But instead of sharing my thoughts, I smiled at Jesse and watched him walk away.

13

I prepped myself for the party. Showered, blew my hair out, and applied actual makeup. Not fun weird makeup like I did for the girl's night out, but understated, ready-for-a-day-at-the-office makeup. As dusk fell and the fairy lights grew stronger and started to make the backyard look magical, I ran out and lit the citronella candles. String lights and candles—perfect atmosphere. Perfect weather. I thanked the island gods. My mom came out, dressed up and made-up as well. We stood at the back deck and took in the sight.

She gave me a sideways hug. "Thanks so much, sweetie. Your aunt would have loved this." I was so glad we had all gotten to this point. It wasn't about us. It was about Aunt Delilah. About everyone who loved her.

Around the corner of the deck walked Penny and Walter, each carrying a platter of food. It looked like baby waffles on shish-kabob sticks. "Where do you want this?" Penny asked.

I rushed over to help. "There's an empty table for the food. Thank you so much; this looks amazing!"

"If you take this, I'll grab some more." Walter handed me the cellophane-covered platter and headed back out front. My mom offered to help and followed him out to the driveway.

"Oh my gosh, are these baby waffles?" My mouth started watering. Had I eaten any pizza at lunch?

"Even when we are trying to make dinner or dessert, we make breakfast." Penny put the platter on the table and pointed to the different types of waffle-kabobs. "Some have bacon, and are savory, some have fruit and are sweet." She took my platter and placed it on the table where she wanted it. "We tried to do pancakes on sticks, but they really just crumble and fall off."

"Breakfast for dinner is my favorite. People will love it." And it felt just quirky enough for a party celebrating my adventurous aunt. I sighed, letting some of the stress go.

"Well, I'm not sure they go with wine, but it's fun."

"Everything goes with wine," Jesse called out from the deck above us, carrying a platter of mini muffins.

Seeing him was a breath of fresh air. I realized I had never seen him in anything other than jeans and a t-shirt. Him in a black dress shirt and leather jacket with dark jeans and black casual shoes was. So. Damn. Sexy.

I gathered him in my arms and thanked him again for all the help, by kissing him hard and long and then breathing the words, "Thank you."

"You know it was a group effort, but if this is the reward, I'll take the credit!"

My mom slipped in with another tray and placed it on the table. "Yes, thank you so much, Jesse, Penny, Walter! And you'll have to tell me who else helped so I can thank them as well." We all walked back up the deck stairs, me to grab the chilling wine, everyone else out front to grab more food. As my mom went around the deck, she asked, "But what if it rains.? We would have had to postpone."

"Nonsense. We have tents at the ready for outdoor events. Unless, of course, a big storm blows in like it did last weekend. *Then* we'd have to postpone ..." Penny's voice faded away until I couldn't hear it anymore.

Aunt Sally was in the kitchen when I pushed the slider closed behind me. She was in all black. Which reminded me that even though this was a celebration for Aunt Del, for Aunt Sally and the islanders—anyone who hadn't come to the funeral—this was also a memorial. Aunt Sally held a tall glass of wine in her hands and gave me a one-armed hug.

"I missed you today—you were on a bike ride?" My heart beat as I thought of how hard it was going to be keeping Sally and my mom separated all night long at the same party.

"I rode around the island, did some hiking, and stayed out of your mom's way. It's not like I like the drama and conflict, although she would say differently." She smiled, softening her jab at my mom.

Right before a whole island of people showed up at my aunt's house wasn't the time to dig into family secrets, but I was tired of being in the dark. Especially since I had found those photo albums and knew that at some point, the three sisters were close. Close enough to be smiling in candid shots. To be easy with each other and want to be together. "So, can you tell me what happened between the three of you?"

"It wasn't the three of us. Del understood. It was just your mom. She holds onto things. But this night is about Del. Not Greta."

I grabbed a few bottles of white wine and Aunt Sally pulled the slider open for me. She grabbed a bottle too and we made our way down to the lawn.

"Well, what would Aunt Del want?" I knew I shouldn't push for more family drama, but it seemed like the right thing to say. To have everyone see tonight through the lens of what would Aunt Del want. I chose my steps carefully on the lawn. All I needed was to stumble over rocks and fall in the backyard. Again.

My aunt said nothing. We put the now sweating wine bottles on the table and went back for more. We could hear the sounds of chattering from the group that went out to get the food. A couple more trips to the refrigerator and the food truck and we were all set up just in time for the guests that started arriving.

One of the first people to arrive was Jack, the older man from the ferry that first day that felt like a year ago. Had it only been a week?

"Hello, Paige. How's your trip going?" Jack hugged me like we were old friends.

Penny floated in with another try of waffle shishkabobs. "What he means to say is: 'Thank you for throwing this party, Paige, your aunt was wonderful.' And then, Jack, let her be. He'll get you telling him your life story if you're not careful, honey." She pulled Jack over to the food table with the promise of bacon. I smiled.

Jesse came over, stood beside me, and handed me glass of wine as I welcomed people onto the lawn. Everyone said at least one nice thing about my aunt and then moved over to the food and wine tables, mingling beside the bar-height tables. The daylight fell enough that the lights started working their magic. An overwhelming feeling of love for my aunt rushed over me.

"She would have loved this." I smiled into Jesse's eyes. "Thank you."

"Stop thanking me. I loved your aunt. Everyone did. Take a look."

Everyone was smiling and hugging and talking. Sharing stories of my aunt and what they loved about her. Some were touching objects in baskets on the table and walking away with something—a book, a hat, a knickknack. There was a lull in people arriving, so Jesse and I walked over to the food table and made up plates. I couldn't wait to try a waffle-kabob.

We put our plates and glasses down at a high top table and I nibbled the waffle on the end of a skewer. It had maple syrup baked in and was just sweet enough. The kabobs I had grabbed had chicken with hot sauce in between the waffles. So yummy. The taste of the food grounded me and I just enjoyed the moment, with Jesse beside me, quietly supporting me.

"These chicken and waffle bites are amazing."

"I should have had something like this for my sister." Jesse was clearly thinking about something else entirely.

And, suddenly things clicked in for me. His showing up all the time, him being at my aunt's house, him seeming to be drawn to me. He wasn't actually drawn to me—he was drawn to working through the feelings of his sister's death. She had died here, at my aunt's house, and he was probably here most of the time for months, nursing her alongside my aunt. And of course, he hadn't worked through it yet. I mean, it had only been a year. Losing a sibling that was your best friend? It could take your whole life to get on the other side of that. Clearly, I was drawn to him because of that loss. Because I was here with a loss of my own. Suddenly everything seemed to be about death. And our quick attraction to one another was completely understandable. We were both dealing with the death of a loved one. I had skirted around this idea earlier, but now I knew for sure. Our relationship wasn't real.

I heard quiet, angry voices coming from the direction of the house. I looked up onto the deck, and saw my mom and Aunt Sally facing off. Aunt Sally had her hands on her hips and my mom had hers crossed in front of her body. I couldn't make out the words, but it didn't look awesome. The last thing this party needed was a family dispute.

Jesse and I exchanged a look—already he could read my expressions—it was too bad that our connection wasn't real. Just situational. He grabbed my hand and we both nonchalantly but quickly strolled up the steps and onto the deck.

"Hey, let's take this inside." Jesse's voice was gentle but commanding. Without another word, my mom and aunt did as they were told.

"What's going on?" I asked as I closed the door behind us.

My mom turned away from us, hands still tight over her body, and I wondered if she was crying.

"She can't get over the past." My aunt roamed the kitchen, washing coffee mugs and setting things right.

"Get over the past? I learned who you were and that I could

never, *never* trust you." My mom's voice quivered with anger laced with pain. I worried she'd break down and didn't know whether giving her a big hug would make it worse.

"I was a kid. I thought my sister was dying. Did I behave well? No. Do I regret it? Yes. I've said 'sorry' for years. YEARS. You can't let us get over it."

"You thought your sister was dying? I thought *I* was dying. And you weren't there." My mom's shoulders shook. I reached out and touched her back, but she pushed my hand away. Jesse took it instead and squeezed.

"We all dealt with your illness in different ways ..."

"It was *my* illness." My mom turned around and jabbed her finger in the air at my aunt. "Me living in a hospital room. Me in danger of dying. Me needing surgeries. And where were you? Living it up in college, living the life I couldn't have. The carefree, normal, healthy college kid. It wasn't just that you didn't visit me or see me or talk with me or help me; you got the life I couldn't. Every day. Showed me all the things I couldn't have or do. Or be. The normal kid."

My aunt turned from the sink and her eyes grew huge.

Silence blanketed the room. My mom, eyes ablaze, continued to tell her truth. "And, I was mature about it. I let it go. I didn't keep you from your niece and nephew. I let you be a part of their lives. But I just couldn't be close to you anymore, after that. We went our separate ways. I don't know why we're drudging this up now." Her anger-filled words were quiet, and I leaned forward to hear her.

"We're drudging this up now because Delilah always wanted us to mend our relationship. And I've wanted that for years now. But you wouldn't let me back in." Aunt Sally rung out the dishtowel she held.

"I couldn't trust you to be there when I needed you—why would I want you in my life? Why would I let you in, only to be disappointed again? To depend on you and have you show me you aren't strong enough?" Tears streamed down my mom's face.

"I made a mistake when I was nineteen. I was self-centered and afraid of my sister dying. I just didn't know how to deal. But it was because I loved you. I couldn't face losing you. And then for the next twenty years, I did lose you; you wouldn't let me in your life at all. I only had one sister. I made my own fear come true. You took yourself out of my life. Haven't I been punished enough?" Sally put the towel down and looked like she wanted to hug her sister, but was waiting for an invitation.

"I just don't understand. How your sister—me—could be lying in a hospital bed and you just check out. Don't come to visit. Don't call." Mom wiped at her tears angrily.

"I was immature. I was self-centered. I was afraid. I'm sorry. And I made sure to be here when Del was dying." Sally took a step closer to my mom.

"You were here?"

"The whole illness. For three months I lived on the island with her when the cancer got bad. That's how I know you called every day. I was here. First with her in the hospital, and then here." Sally gestured around the room.

"She never told me. You were here at the end?" My mom took a step toward my aunt.

"I was here at the end. I know you missed it by a few days, but you had already said your goodbyes, and that was okay. But I was here. And every moment of her illness reminded me how I had let you down. Every minute made we want to change the past. To have been there for you."

They both had tears streaming down their faces. I leaned back into Jesse and he put his arms around me.

"You regret not being there for me?"

Sally closed the gap and gathered my mom in her arms. "Every moment, I regret that. But I can't go back in time, and I can never make it up to you."

"You were here for Delilah in the end?" My mom clung to her sister fiercely.

"I was here for her. It took a whole lifetime, but I wasn't about to make that mistake again. You were right to think the worst of me—I did." Sally rubbed her sister's back.

"I'm sorry. I just didn't know how to forgive you. Honestly I didn't want to. It was easier to be mad at you." My mom returned the back rub.

"You don't have to be sorry. I'm the one who's sorry. I couldn't deal with the idea of you not being in my life, but I made it so you couldn't be in my life. I should have been more mature." Sally's voice was filled with sadness, but also some hope.

"I should have let Del bring us back together. I was stubborn." My mom pulled Sally back, out of the hug, and held her at arm's length. Then she smiled the biggest smile I had ever seen.

"She did bring us back together." Sally grinned at my mom, and then at me. She gestured to me, and I rushed over to hug them, letting my own tears fall.

I heard the slider quietly open and shut and knew Jesse was giving us space. Space to finally be a family.

14

We were a united family for the first time in my life as we walked back out to the party, after we spent some moments catching up for real and collecting ourselves. When I walked down onto the lawn, with my mom and aunt beside me, Jesse gave me a big grin. What I wouldn't give for him to truly be interested in me; for me to have met him under different circumstances.

I raised a glass of wine in the air when I got to the tables. I didn't even need to bang on it with a piece of silverware, the crowd was waiting for a speech.

"Thank you so much for coming. Everything about this party is *so* Aunt Del. She was all about bringing people together in community. She would love this party. All walks of her life together. Celebrating. And tonight, she has finally done what I think she might have been trying to do her whole life. Bring her two sisters back together. She was never one to rush anything or anyone; she always let people come to things on their own terms. In that way she respected people and let them be who they are. And I loved that she treated everyone that she met like they were the most important and special person."

I surveyed the crowd, bathed in soft light, with open and

loving faces. "She leaves us all with that. Thank you to everyone who donated and helped out tonight: Margo and Drew at Magnolias; Penny and Walter from the cafe, Xavier, Bells, and Jesse for all the work and setup.

"Thank you to everyone for loving my aunt and being here to celebrate. Make sure to grab one of Aunt Del's books or something to remember her by and sign the guestbook."

I smiled to the crowd, even as my voice broke a little. "Let's toast to her amazing life. To Aunt Del. Living forever in our hearts." I raised my glass even higher.

The crowed mirrored me and then people started yelling out, "To Delilah." Tears started streaming down my face again, but they were tears of relief and love this time. The sounds of clinking glasses filled the air.

When there was silence again I said, "I'd love to open the floor to anyone who wants to share a story about Delilah."

Surprisingly, and awesomely, my mom launched into a story about Delilah as a girl, and even more surprisingly, Aunt Sally tag-teamed with her on the story, adding funny bits. They were like a comedy duo and I couldn't believe that forty years of animosity could vanish in a moment. That was the miracle of my Aunt Delilah.

I wished their reunion could have taken place while Aunt Del was still here, but I shoved that thought away. It was wonderful that it was happening at all, and I had to believe that Aunt Del was somehow watching it unfold. I looked past the Edison lights strung above us and into the sky. I whispered, "Thanks, Aunt Del."

A woman slipped out of the shadows, and I recognized Aunt Delilah's girlfriend, Sylvi. She walked to me, her face beaming. "Your mom and Sally?"

"I know, right?"

"Honey, this is beautiful. I couldn't face well ... the island, without her, but had to come and see this party." Sylvi took my shoulders in her hands and her face grew stern. "You are amazing. Never forget that. There is no better gift to Del than what you did here today—bringing her sisters back together. Bringing me back to the island. Bringing everyone together. Thank you."

She pulled me into a hug and I couldn't help but burst into tears. The weight that had been on my shoulders since I had heard I was in charge of my aunt's house and belongings dissolved in an instant. Sylvi broke the embrace, wiping the tears from my face. "Your aunt was *so proud* of you, and she would be even more proud of you today."

I nodded, unable to speak. Sylvi nodded too, as if she was satisfied her message had gotten through to me, and then turned toward the speakers at the front of the lawn.

I stood next to her, trying to get my emotions under control. It took a couple of shaky breaths, a couple of large gulps of wine, and a couple of bites of the waffle kabob someone had thrust into my hand.

Jesse came over and pulled me into his side, nodding at Sylvi. The three of us watched and listened and enjoyed all the Aunt Del stories. They ranged from impish pranks recounted by friends to gratitude from her patients.

Someone hovered in the back, in the shadows, and I watched them get closer before I recognized who it was. Frank. Of course. As I scanned the back end of the crowd, I saw my brother there too, and my assistant, Sheila, as well as Cynthia.

As soon as the stories died down and the toasting ended and people started mingling again, laughing and crying, I excused myself and Jesse, and we wandered to the back, with me yelling to my brother as we walked, realizing that I might be a tad bit tipsy.

I grabbed him into a hug, hugged Sheila and Cyn, and introduced them to Jesse. "I'm so glad you're all here," I yelled. Feeling immediately guilty, since my brother should have been standing up at the front. I didn't even know when he had gotten in.

"Hey, sis. This is all amazing." He swept his arm over the crowd. "You know I would have helped, right?"

"It all sort-of happened. Del's friends did all the heavy-lifting." I looked at the guests and a number of faces were turned toward me, waiting to catch my eye and wave. I felt the love all around.

"What the hell happened between Mom and Aunt Sally? I can't believe they're in the same space, let alone doing that!" He pointed to them hugging one another and chatting up the crowd.

I filled him and my friends in on what had happened earlier.

Mick seemed stunned. "A lifetime of family drama erased in an afternoon? You're a miracle worker."

"I think Aunt Del gets the win. Mom and Sally said that she tried to bring them back together her entire life. I think she finally did."

We stood in silence for a moment, and I thought of how I always tried to do everything on my own; I even tried to take care of my aunt's belongings on my own. But how much better everything was when I let her friends help.

"This is so much more than I could have done by myself. Look at what happens when we all come together. Aunt Del was all about doing things together. Maybe I need to take a page out of her book more often." I impetuously pulled my friends, Jesse, and my brother into a group hug. "You all are amazing for being here. When did you get in?"

I dropped my arms and we stopped hugging, but stayed close, like we were in a huddle.

My brother and Sheila answered together. "The seven o'clock ferry."

Sheila giggled, and said, "The three of us spotted each other in the line for the ferry and talked the whole way out."

Frank materialized out of the shadows and pushed into our little circle. Cyn scooted closer to me, her hand on my back. Jesse pulled me in front of him, his arms protectively around me..

Cynthia spat out, "Frank, why the hell are you here?"

I loved Cynthia for her straightforwardness. She and I had become best friends in the weeks after we found out Frank was cheating on me *with* her.

When Frank just looked angrily at Cynthia, I spoke up. "He's going through something and came to talk with me."

I could see Jesse inspecting Cynthia's face closely, and I wondered if they would compare notes later.

"Well, it's impossible to get Paige to answer my texts and calls, so I had to come out and see her."

"Get a clue, Frank. She's your ex. If she doesn't pick up, she doesn't want to talk to you." Cyn's words sounded like a warning.

Bells arrived to the group with a chipper, "Hello!"

I put my hand out to stop Frank who looked like he was going to yell at Cyn. "Um, Frank's also had a death in the family and needed some support."

"Well, Frank can find that support somewhere other than the ex he verbally abused for a year." Cyn stepped between me and Frank.

Oh my god, things were going from miraculous-family-reunion to friend-brawl quickly. At the words "verbally abused," Jesse, my brother, and Bells pulled themselves up tall like things were going to get physical in a second. Sheila looked super uncomfortable, and Cyn smiled. Big. Clearly, she had the backup she needed for whatever rash thing she was planning to do next.

A rash thing I had to prevent from happening.

"Everyone, this is a memorial for Aunt Del. Let's remember where we are," I pleaded.

"The only person here trying to make it about himself is this jackass here." Cyn wasn't backing down. She never backed down. Ever.

"Okay, okay. Give me a minute with Frank." The only way to diffuse the situation was to get Frank away from Jesse, my friends, and my brother.

"See? Frank gets what he wants." Cyn shook her head like she wouldn't let it happen.

I glared at Cyn and she glared back. I put my hand out to stop anyone from following me. I pulled Frank away from the party and all the way around the front of the house.

"Frank, they're right—this night is about my aunt. It's about the family being together and my mom and aunt just reunited. Why don't you go back to your hotel and I'll come by after the party?"

"I've been here for days and you keep ducking me." He tried to take my hand, but I pulled away.

"I'm sorry. I just have been dealing with family things. That's why I'm here." I stopped walking and squared off with him.

"You're throwing parties." His voice sounded more whiny than I remembered.

"Yes. I am. Memorial parties for my aunt." I started to feel angry. Frank was belittling my things just like he did during the end of our relationship.

"And picnics at lighthouses," he spat out.

I looked at him. "Have you been following me?" For some reason, a chill went down my spine. For all the things we went through—all the times he treated me in a manner that was all about him—he'd never done anything that seemed off. He had always just seemed needy. I didn't wait for his answer, because it was already clear. "I'm going back to my aunt's party. This is over between us. I'm sorry about your mom, but you need to lean on someone else. Not me. Go home, Frank." I turned to go back to the party.

He grabbed my arm. "I need *you*. You're the only one ..."

I pulled my arm away. In a low but harsh tone, I told him, "Get your hands off me."

Suddenly the fact that we were standing in the shadows where nobody else could see us felt scary.

It's only Frank. Nothing to be scared about. But I couldn't convince myself. I repeated, "Go home, Frank."

I bolted back to the party and arrived at my group of friends breathless. Jesse looked wildly concerned. "Are you okay?"

I smiled shakily at their faces, bathed in the fairy lights.

"Totally fine. I told him to leave." Even so, I was surprised he wasn't following me back to the party. His persistence suddenly felt alarming.

My brother's eyes scanned the dark behind me. "He better listen to you. If I see him ..."

"We were just about to follow you and Frank, make sure everything was, you know, okay." Cyn nodded, seemingly as concerned as I was.

I searched her face. Wondering if I should ask her if she thought Frank could be moved to violence. Instinctual alarm bells were still going off from that moment with him. I had never seen him act anything remotely like that before. He had been an asshole, sure, but never angry or aggressive.

"Anyone need another glass of wine?" I made a move to go grab everyone another round of drinks, but Jesse put his hand on my arm. The difference in the touch compared to Frank's angry grab was immense. He radiated care and concern. Too bad he only liked me because we were both going through the losses. Because I could get used to that.

"I'll grab drinks for everyone. You stay and enjoy spending time with your brother and friends." He smiled at me and I smiled back at him, even more regretful that this couldn't be real between us.

The rest of the evening passed in a blur of feelings. Feelings of gratitude that my Aunt Sally and Mom made up slipped into feelings of renewed sadness for losing Aunt Delilah. I allowed the stories and memories of my aunt to wash over me when someone new came up to talk to me. Pretty soon I was hugging everyone and crying and feeling so connected to this place and my aunt's life.

I had thought that I had come to terms with her death at her funeral, but I realized that the grief of her loss was something I would never really get over. I couldn't really control it, and even though I really liked to control things, it was going to have to be okay to just ride the rollercoaster and feel what I was feeling.

My friends, old and new, took it upon themselves to make sure my aunt, my mom, and my brother were okay the whole party.

Finally, after everyone left, and the remnants of waffle-kabobs and wine glasses were cleaned up, we all sat in the library. My mom and Aunt Sally looked exhausted but so happy, sitting together on the loveseat. Cynthia, Sheila, and Mick shared the couch, while I sat in a chair with Jesse balanced on the arm. Bells stood, talking animatedly, mostly with her arms.

Aunt Sally raised her wine glass which was now filled with water (after Nellie reminded us all to hydrate before she left), and said, "To endings and new beginnings. To family, and to friends who are family." We all cheered and then said goodnight, as she ambled off to the downstairs guest room.

"Sheila and Cynthia, grab your stuff. Mick, you can stay upstairs in the pull-out bed in the office. Sheila and Cyn, you'll bunk with me in Aunt Del's room."

Sheila shook her head. "I'm fine grabbing a room somewhere."

"It's after midnight. I don't want you moped-ing around the island looking for a place to stay." I stood and stretched.

"They can stay in the office—I can find a room elsewhere."

"Nobody is getting a room. You all are staying here. Aunt Del would have insisted. So, I'm insisting." I yawned, suddenly and completely worn out.

They couldn't argue with that. Everyone slowly moved toward rooms. "Bells and Jesse—do you want to crash on these couches?"

"I think we should let this be a family thing. Thanks for the great party." Bells gave me a hug. "Your aunt was amazing and so are you."

"Are you okay to drive your moped?"

"Sure am. I've been drinking water for the last hour or so. I'm good." Bells hugged everyone, including my brother, and then yelled out, "Toodle-loo, everyone." She headed out the door.

I cleared things to the kitchen and Jesse helped. Once we were alone in the kitchen, he took me into his arms. I felt carved out inside and exhausted. Between the family reconciliation, the memorial for my aunt, and throwing Frank out of the party, I was spent.

Jesse tenderly rocked me, one arm around my body, one protectively holding my head to his shoulder. I knew I should talk to him about what I had decided: I was heading back to mainland life, because I knew he only felt close to me because my aunt's death reminded him of his sister's passing, but I didn't have it in me. I was totally leading him on by letting him comfort me.

"Please forgive me," I murmured into his shirt.

"Shhhh. It's okay." He held me tight.

I heard water running upstairs as people got ready for bed, and I stared at the fairy lights outside.

"Want me to unplug all those?" Jesse untangled himself from me and followed my gaze.

"No, I love them. There's something so magical about string lights." I swayed on my feet.

"Your aunt would have loved tonight." Jesse pulled me back into his arms.

"I think it was a fitting goodbye, although I'm not sure I'm ready to say goodbye to her." Jesse's touch made me feel so safe.

"I don't think you need to say goodbye until you are ready. And I'm realizing that even when we think we've said goodbye, that people live in our hearts regardless."

That was nice. Even though I shouldn't, I cozied back into his arms. Which was going to make everything worse tomorrow when I had to tell him I couldn't see him anymore. But I ignored that thought and was selfish and just let him rock me and comfort me. I closed my eyes. Drifted a little bit.

"Babe?" He shuffled us toward the stairs. "You awake?"

I murmured something. I wasn't even sure what it was. He half-guided, half-carried me upstairs and knocked on the bedroom door.

Sheila opened it. Cyn waved from the bathroom door, her toothbrush in her mouth.

"She's asleep on her feet."

"Hey sweety, time for bed," Sheila said, moving away so we could enter the room.

I left the warmth of Jesse's body and staggered toward the bathroom, waving a hand behind me. "Bye, Jesse, thanks." Then I ran a toothbrush over my teeth, splashed water on my face, and stumbled back to the bedroom and into bed.

Both Cynthia and Sheila snickered at me before someone turned out the light.

"Sleep well," Jesse whispered. It was sweet that he waited to see me tucked into bed before closing the door behind him. A moment later his truck started up outside.

And even though I knew I was going to have to break up with him tomorrow, I held onto the safe feeling of being in his arms.

"Bye, Aunt Del." And even though that was a ridiculous thing to say into the darkness, Sheila repeated it. "Bye, Paige's Aunt Del. You are well-loved." Cyn said, "Damn straight."

And instead of making me feel sad, that made me burst with pride.

"And, boy, Jesse is hot, Paige. Nice work," Sheila added.

I giggled in spite of myself, and soon we were laughing with abandon. Until my mom called out like we were three middle schoolers at a sleepover, "That's enough, girls, settle down!"

Which only made us laugh harder.

Was everything going to be okay after all?

I was too tired to find and consult my Magic Eight Ball.

15

Sheila poked me and I giggled, remembering talking late into the night. The room was bright with sunlight when I opened my eyes. Water was running in the bathroom; Cynthia was already in the shower.

"So, this place is amazing. I can't believe your aunt lived here. It's like a vacation."

"And you've only seen it after dark. Wait until I show you around in the daylight!"

And then Sheila wanted to talk about work, which I immediately put a stop to since it was sorta vacation. And since I needed coffee, immediately.

We got dressed quickly and went down to the kitchen. Mick was up and in pajamas and no shirt making coffee, and Sheila gave him a long look. If my brother wasn't already engaged to his boyfriend, Jinx, I might have thought about setting them up. Now who was shipping people? We all grabbed coffee and went out onto the deck to enjoy the early morning sun.

Birds twittered and the day looked new. New like it had been washed clean with a storm, even though it hadn't. I leaned on the railing, looking back into the kitchen at my mom and Sally scooting around the kitchen, talking and laughing together.

Warmth rushed over me. I couldn't believe that broken relationship had been mended.

I surveyed the damage from the night before and realized that not only did our island friends put on this amazing party, but they cleaned up as well. There were empty tables set up and the strings of lights, but that was it.

My phone buzzed and I closed my eyes and hoped that it was something that I had the strength to deal with. And then I opened them when I realized I had the strength of all these women behind me. Behind me? Inside me. Including my aunt. The feeling of being in her presence washed over me. I sighed a giant sigh and turned my face to the sun. Everything was going to be alright.

I checked my phone.

I'm on the island — Matt

Oh my god, Matt was here! I didn't know how, or why. He should be in Texas. The one-night stand we had when I discovered that Frank was cheating turned into a relationship until he had to move to start a teaching job.

And then I realized that it was me who felt clean inside, not that the island felt washed. I was excited to see Matt.

Why? How?

For you, silly. And a plane ride. It's break at school. Mick called me about the memorial.

It was last night. Beautiful.

I know. I stopped in.

What? When?

I saw you talking with Frank, and realized that he was doing the same thing as he did at your aunt's funeral. So, I escorted him back to his hotel.

Thank you.

I slipped into a chair and just felt love for these amazing friends and for Matt—what had I done to deserve such loyalty and love?

Can you come over? I'd love to see you.

Sure. I'll moped over.

I didn't know what I felt about that, aside from happiness.

My mom and Sally joined us, bringing leftover pastries out on paper plates. We were all silent, eating and drinking coffee, but it was a nice silence. A peaceful silence.

We planned a day of exploring the island: going on a hike on some nature trails that ended up on the bluffs. We had a collection of mopeds to use since Cyn, Sheila, and my brother had each rented one when they got on the island the night before. Sally and my mom decided to go on their own and catch up while biking the island.

Jesse texted, and I invited him along, even though my heart sank. At some point, I'd have to tell him we were going our separate ways. My brother called a real estate agent on the island to come by and take pictures of my aunt's now empty-ish house. It was time to sell and move on, back to my real life in Boston. I read people's stories about my aunt in the guest book from the party while Sheila, Cynthia, and my brother made peanut butter sandwiches and packed up a picnic lunch for us all to share while hiking. I was happy to see some of the waffle kabobs make it into the lunch bags.

I read a particularly stirring story that Jack wrote about the care my aunt gave him after surgery. Constant house visits, and lunches together, while my aunt made sure that he was living life after surgery well. The first person I had met on the island attributed my aunt for saving his life. I sighed again. My aunt's legacy would live on for years.

Cyn yelled words I couldn't quite make out, and I closed the book tenderly before rushing out to the front yard. Matt had arrived, with pastries from Penny and Walter. Of course. Because they hadn't donated enough food last night.

Matt handed off the boxes and turned to me, gathering me into his arms. I knew instantly that what we had wasn't romantic anymore. I felt safe in his arms, for sure, but I no longer felt the whole-body reaction like I felt with Jesse.

Matt held me at arm's length. "You look really good."

"You too." Whatever he was doing in Texas was working for him. His skin was tanned and he looked even more muscular than when he had left. If that was even possible.

"I'm a part of a great team at the local fire station. Not sure about the teaching part of things—there's a ton of bureaucracy—but the kids are great. We'll see if it's for me."

I looked around. We were alone. Everyone had left to let us to catch up. Matt pulled me closer and touched his forehead to mine. I closed my eyes. Feeling the warm sun on my back, hearing the birds call to one another, and just breathing in the day.

We separated and Matt led me to the porch, where we sat on a rocking love seat.

I put my head on his shoulder and gazed off down the dirt driveway surrounded by trees. I asked him questions about Texas, and he gently asked me questions about my aunt. We were both surprised at how okay I was. I was also surprised at how great it felt to just be friends with Matt. He asked me about my love life, and I told him about Jesse. About how he was great, but wouldn't fit into my life back in Boston. He nodded. That was, after all, why Matt and I had called it quits. The long-distance thing. He told me he had dated another teacher but it hadn't gone anywhere.

A truck pulled into the driveway and Jesse hopped out. My smile turned into a frown. At some point today, I was going to have to be clear. Jesse and I weren't going to become anything. My mind didn't get the message, and as Jesse strode toward us, all I could think of was the sun on his naked body. I was in full-on flush as he vaulted the steps and noticed me cozying up to Matt.

He didn't even flinch. I had to give him a lot of credit. I stood, pulling Matt to his feet.

"Matt, this is Jesse. Jesse, Matt." They both shook hands, and both appeared to be sizing each other up.

"Sis, we're all packed up ..." Mick's voice faded away as he took the scene in, and then came back strong. "Matt! Great to see you, man."

Matt stuck out his hand for another round of manly handshaking, but Mick pulled him into a bear hug.

"How's Jinx? How's life as an engaged guy?" Matt slapped Mick on the back before letting him go.

"Pretty damn amazing. How long have you been on the island?" Mick grinned.

"I got in last night. Flew into Connecticut and took the last ferry out. Unfortunately, I have to leave tonight. Quick visit."

"You missed a great party." Jesse nodded at me.

"He was actually here, but didn't stay," I said.

"I saw Frank refusing to take no for an answer, and so I took him back to his hotel."

"Thanks." From both Mick and Jesse. I rolled my eyes, and then the three men turned on me.

It's like I could read their minds and they were all thinking the same thing. I put my arms up in mock surrender. "I've been straight with Frank. Completely transparent. Not my fault that he keeps popping up. He's harmless, though." I hoped.

From the thin line of Jesse's lips, I could tell he didn't believe that. Mick and Matt exchanged glances and suddenly the three of them, without speaking, were on one team. I rolled my eyes yet again. There was nothing like three well-meaning men to get in the way of a woman trying to live her life.

I mean, Jesse was completely hot, looking all protectively at me. It was just misplaced. I didn't need them to take care of me, at all.

"Hey y'all, we're all packed up. Ready to ..." Cyn bounced out of the screen door and stopped completely. "Ooooh, threesome and your brother. Kinky."

I swatted her and chased her back into the house. "So. Inappropriate. Cynthia!"

After filling water bottles, and loading the suitcases of everyone leaving at the end of the day onto Jesse's truck, we were off.

The island spread before us like there were new adventures

around every corner. The road wound around the perimeter and the views of craggy shoreline down to crashing waves were spectacular. We passed my aunt and mom and got to the trailhead first. Jesse lounged next to his truck and we all gathered to wait for the bikers.

The hike through the lush spring green growth was super fun. The day warmed and we had a spirited lunch catching up and hearing more about the island from Jesse. We planned to have a fun dinner out before most everyone took the seven o'clock ferry home.

Everyone packed their stuff up, we returned my brother and Sheila's mopeds and did a little shopping on the main strip, while my brother and I excused ourselves to take to a real estate agent. Jesse got us reservations at the Boathouse restaurant overlooking the beach and ferry dock. We got everything sorted just in time to walk over to the restaurant.

We invited Bells, Margo, Drew, Penny, and Walter to dinner to thank them for all the help and donations to the party. Walter wasn't feeling great, so he and Penny didn't come. It was still a full and rowdy table out on the deck of the restaurant. I read more from the guest book and we toasted to my aunt a lot. Before we knew it, it was time to say goodbye. Jesse and I said goodbye to Bells, Margo, and Drew, before walking my mom, my aunt, Sheila, Cynthia, Matt, and my brother to the ferry. We watched as they got on, and the ferry blasted its horn and pulled away. We waved like maniacs on the shore.

A feeling of completion washed over me. The party was done, my aunt's stuff sorted, and the real estate agent all set up. My time at the island was over and seeing my family and friends leave brought that home for me. I would go back to an empty house tonight—empty of my aunt and her things; empty of my family and friends. It was time to move on. Way past time to move on.

"How are you doing?" Jesse pulled out a plank from the back of his truck like a ramp, pushed my moped into the bed of his truck, and then walked me around his truck and put me inside, then hopping in himself.

All the lights hanging outside the strip of shops and restaurants and hotels on the main strip made it look inviting and special—like it was always a party. Even though the party was over for me.

"I'm feeling like all this is final. I'm sad, but it feels right. Like we finally gave Aunt Del the send-off that she should have. And she brought her sisters together. It feels right," I repeated.

"Do you want to go to the bar and grab a drink? Talk about it?" Jesse held my hand.

"I'm so tired. I just want to crash. Would you mind taking me to my aunt's house?"

"Of course." He let go of my hand and massaged the back of my neck.

I pulled away. Mainly because it felt great and I knew I shouldn't feel that way. I should be honest and let him know. "Jesse ..."

"That was a lot of goodbyes just now."

I stared at the strip of shops as we pulled out of the parking lot. I straightened up as I spotted someone who looked a lot like Frank from the back. Was I seeing things, or had he not left the island yet?

My thoughts turned to Frank and the breakup—it had been really bad. I should start that process with Jesse.

"So, I'm leaving tomorrow." I kept my gaze securely out the window.

"When will you be back?" he asked.

Suddenly that question exhausted me. The week had been exhausting. Cathartic in some ways where my family was concerned, but exhausting. All I wanted was not to be having this conversation. I wanted to crawl into bed and ignore the fact that I was planning on saying a final goodbye to Jesse. That I would sell my aunt's house and close this chapter of my life.

Jesse would have to come to grips with the fact that he was

only drawn to me because of the situation. Probably as soon as I was gone, he'd realize that his feelings toward me were misplaced. But I was too tired to get into it tonight.

"I don't know. I can't plan more than what I'm doing tomorrow." I stared out the window, not paying any attention to the island views.

"Do me a favor? Don't make any life decisions right now," Jesse said.

"Like what?" I turned to him.

"Like selling your aunt's house." He kept his eyes glued to the road.

I studied the side of his face as he turned down my aunt's long driveway. "Why not? It's not meant to be my house. Why wouldn't I sell?"

"Maybe you want a place to stay of your own when you come back here."

"If I want to come back, I can stay at the Inn. I don't need a whole house." Why were we even talking about this?

"But it's your aunt's house. Every time you visit, you'll remember her. It's comforting, right?"

"I think it's comforting for you." I didn't know where the edge to my voice came from. Or maybe I did. I was so just tired.

"Comforting for me?"

"If you want to remember your sister, you can buy my aunt's house. Not saddle me with a vacation property."

We pulled into the parking space in front of my aunt's house.

"What? Where is this coming from?"

"I'm just tired. And ready to finish my duty to my aunt. Go back to my real life. You should understand. You're finishing your sister's house, right?" What was I saying? Why was I bringing his sister into it? This was not the way to tell him I thought he only wanted me in his life because of my connection to my aunt and his sister's death. "I'm ready for closure."

"You want closure? From me? You want to leave the island and not come back?"

"That's not what I meant." Was it? I mean, that was what I wanted right? I just didn't want this to happen right now, like this. I wanted to be better at letting him down. Clearly I didn't break things off well. Maybe if I had been clearer with Frank, maybe he could have let me go instead of stalking me on an island at my aunt's memorial party. Although a little voice in the back of my head stated that I had been clear with Frank.

Jesse sat and stared at me, his expression getting darker and darker.

"Look, I'm just tired," I repeated when I couldn't think of anything else to say. I stared at my aunt's dark house and suddenly wanted two things with equal force: to break down and cry, and to be far away from Jesse. Because I didn't want to break down right now and being close to him was making me feel like a pressure cooker, like I was going to explode. "And we are just together because of our losses. We've both lost people," I stated.

"You think that I only have feelings for you because of my sister's death? What kind of screwed-up logic is that?" Jesse's voice was so angry. I had never heard him angry before.

Hot tears welled up behind my eyes and I knew I had to get away before they boiled over. "I don't know. I just need to be alone."

I jumped out of the truck and ran into the house, locking the door behind me, listening to him peel out and drive away.

I wished I could do that too—just drive off this island and be back home in my apartment. I stumbled up the stairs and crawled into my aunt's bed, not bothering to brush my teeth or wash my face. Then the sobs came. Alone in my aunt's house, knowing that our goodbye was right, but final.

★★★

Even though I hadn't slept well, I was up early, showered and packed, before the real estate agent, Martin, showed up to put up signs and take pictures. I knew I should talk to Jesse, but maybe it would be better to get back to my real life and then call and officially break up with him. I didn't know if that was the coward's way out, or if that was the sensible way out. More and more I was feeling like the island had cast a spell over me. Better to shake off the island magic and then talk to Jesse. Plus, he had been really angry last night when I suggested that he didn't really like me for me. Really angry.

I texted Bells that I was heading to the mainland on the ferry and could she arrange to have the tables returned? She answered that she would be happy to do it, asked when was I going to be back. I texted that I didn't know. I'd have to look at my work schedule.

I wandered around the house one more time and had one last cup of coffee on the back deck. Then I made sure everything was clean and put away—I'd come back and figure out what to do with the big items, like furniture, once the house sold. I threw out all the perishables leftover from the party, tossing one last waffle bite into my mouth. Maybe I'd have one last meal at the Oceanside Cafe to say goodbye to Penny. I took out the trash and locked up. Stashed all my Aunt's outside furniture back into the shed and locked that as well. Wheeled my suitcase outside and looked around for my rented moped.

Oh my gosh. It was in the back of Jesse's truck. So much for my plan of leaving without confronting Jesse's faux feelings for me. Unless I texted Xavier to pick me up. But that felt really cowardly. I needed to return the moped, regardless of whether I was ready to truly end things with Jesse.

I wheeled my suitcase onto the shade of the porch and texted Jesse.

Hey—sorry, but my moped is in your truck.

His response: **That's what you're sorry for?**

Um, yes.

I stared at the three dots for a while, waiting for his response. Finally:

I can stop by on my lunch break and drop it to you.

I checked my watch. It was already 11:30, and it wasn't like I could walk to the ferry dock, dragging a suitcase behind me. I sighed.

Thanks! That would be great!

I faked enthusiasm in my text, pressed send, and dragged my suitcase to the porch.

I looked up at the angry clouds rolling in and asked my Magic Eight Ball why the romance gods were throwing me this kind of curveball.

ASK AGAIN LATER.

16

I grew more and more anxious, waiting for Jesse to arrive.

Suddenly I felt back in the life I left with Frank. Those days when I had let Frank take over more and more of my life and he seemed in charge of everything. I had vowed to never let a guy rule my life that much and had practiced good boundaries and everything.

And then I had left the moped in Jesse's truck and now I was at his mercy to get me back home. And he had been pretty angry last night. I didn't want to be around someone that angry again. I just wanted peace.

All the late-night crying had left me exhausted, yet again. I didn't think I had the reserves to say what I needed to say. I was pretty sure everything was going to come out wrong and I was going to make a mess of things.

And Jesse had only been kind and considerate to me. So even if his feelings for me were a product of losing his sister and the connection to my aunt, he didn't deserve anything other than my A-game when it came to breaking up with him.

I heard the truck before I saw it and wheeled my suitcase back to the front of the house.

"Really?" Jesse's voice sounded even angrier than last night. He pointed at the thing offending him: the for-sale sign in front of my aunt's house. I wrestled my suitcase into the back seat even while he got out to help me.

"I'm good," I said, wishing that were true.

He opened the side door open for me after I got my suitcase in the back and closed me in his truck. I watched him walk around the front and wondered what he was thinking. Regardless of what he was thinking, I owed it to him to rip off the Band-Aid.

"Look, we've only known each other a week, we've both been dealing with big losses, and I need to get back to my real life."

Jesse drove out of my aunt's driveway and onto the street, not saying anything at all. Silence grew. So did my anxiety.

"I mean, it was fun."

Silence.

"I'll always remember this time. Thank you."

Silence.

And he turned left instead of the right that would take us into town.

"Um, I wanted to take the one pm ferry."

He finally turned to me. "I want to show you something."

He pulled the truck onto an overlook parking lot, and parked, with a spectacular view of cliffs down to the ocean. "This is my favorite view."

I nodded. "It's lovely."

"It's my favorite. My sister preferred the lush green of the bog in front of the distant views of the ocean. I think it felt more protected; safer. But I like this view. You can't hide from the wildness of nature. The wildness of the ocean."

As if on cue, clouds crowded out the sun and the day darkened. Sheets of dark rain hit the ocean just beyond the island, and it looked like it was heading our way. I'd leave this place as I had come to it: in a rainstorm.

"I don't ..."

"Just let me finish." His voice was soft and not at all angry.

"I don't have feelings for you just because I lost my sister. I'm not lost in my grief. I care for you because of who you are. Because you wandered out into a storm to make things right at your aunt's house. Because you stayed to throw an impromptu party so that friends of your aunt could have closure. Because you helped your mom and aunt to reconcile. Because you let people be who they are and you love them for it."

I opened my mouth to speak, but he put a hand up. I watched the rain sweep onto the beach instead.

"Losing my sister is a part of this, though. Because it made me realize how short life can be. How I can't just sit on the sidelines when I feel something real. And what I feel toward you is real."

Rain pelted the car and the windshield wipers started up. I watched them rhythmically sweep the windshield. I was tired, confused, and didn't want to open myself up right now. I had done that so much this week, felt so much, and I knew my emotional wires got crossed.

And even though Jesse was saying otherwise, I felt like his were crossed too. He thought he liked me, but I wasn't sure. And I couldn't move my whole life to an island for crossed emotions. But how could I say that to him? How could I make him see it? All I could do was try.

"So much has changed this week. I feel both untethered and also like I understand so much more about my family. I need some time to piece those things together. I don't think it's the right time for me to follow a vacation romance."

"You mean you don't want to follow your heart."

"I mean, look at what Frank is going through—I've got to be responsible for that on some level."

"You're not responsible for what some dick does."

"He's not a ..."

"Look, respect me enough to hear that my feelings for you are real. I want to explore this." He grabbed my hand in his and we turned toward each other. His touch zinged electricity throughout my body, making me remember all the moments we had touched before, and I wished I could just ignore real life and follow that feeling. It felt good. So good.

"I need to go back to my real life. This is only a hiatus for me."

He moved his hands over my arms and held my face in both hands. "This is real life. How can I convince you?"

I was having a hard time thinking; a hard time breathing. He was so close and my whole body wanted him even closer. Touching me. The rain outside made it feel like we were the only two people on earth.

My voice came out in a whisper. "This isn't *my* real life."

It was like I burned him. He dropped my face, jolted back in his seat, put the truck in reverse, and pulled back onto the street.

"I'm sorry," I whispered between the shushing sounds of the wipers pushing the water off the windshield.

He didn't say anything at all. We drove quietly to town, and I kept my gaze outside at the rain-blown trees and tall grass.

Nicely done, Paige. I didn't feel anything at all, though. So, I *knew* my reaction was right. It's better to let him down now rather than string him along. Better to end things before they got messy, like they did with Frank.

We pulled up to the ferry dock ten minutes before one. Too late for me to return the moped and still make the ferry.

I hopped out and to the back of the truck bed. Jesse was there already and put his hand on the tailgate, not letting me open it.

"I've got it." His voice was commanding and angry.

"Okay." I stood back and waited for him to take the moped out. He didn't move. We both got wet in the rain.

"Go get your ferry."

"I have to return the moped."

"I said, I've got it."

Oh. I stood there stupidly.

"Go get your ferry."

I dragged my suitcase out of the back of the truck. I couldn't leave things like this. I wanted to say goodbye. A good goodbye. I was sorry and cared for him. I just didn't want to lead him on when our feelings for each other weren't real.

Impulsively, I ran around the car and smack into him, kissing him deeply and surely. As suddenly as I had pushed myself into his body, I pushed away from him and ran down through the driving rain to the line of people waiting to embark. With moments to spare, I was on the ferry.

The ferry sounded its horn and backed off from the dock. I pulled my aunt's raincoat tighter around myself and headed up to the top deck, wondering if Jesse was watching the boat leave. But when I looked out to his parking spot, it was empty. As it should have been. I had ended things; I didn't want him waiting around watching me leave. The island shrunk from view. When there was no land left to see, I headed inside the small cabin for some lunch.

I felt nothing. The peaceful feeling after my aunt's party had left me and I was just numb. It also felt like I had been gone from my life forever, not just a week. Like I was a satellite and was now in a completely different orbit. My phone buzzed and before I could even consider who it might be, I realized I hoped it was Jesse. It wasn't. It was my brother saying he had made it home and wondering how I was doing. Then Cyn and Sheila texted along with my mom and my aunt. I slipped into the comfort of focusing on my phone and letting them know I was on my way home. Then I settled back in my seat and let the exhaustion wash over me.

The rising and dipping of the ferry in the stormy sea almost lulled me to sleep before we got to the mainland. When it docked, I shuffled off the boat and down the steps and tried to remember where I parked my car a lifetime ago.

Finally, I retraced my steps and found it. It had a parking ticket on it because I had forgotten to re-up the parking pass on the app when I stayed longer than expected on the island. I grabbed the parking ticket off the windshield and walked to the trunk, sliding in the mud puddles. I opened the trunk, but as I picked up my suitcase, my feet slid in the mud and I landed on my back behind the car. My suitcase bounced off me and into a deep puddle, splashing me.

I lay, face turned up to the sky, feeling the wet seep into my clothes from the puddle beneath me and the rain showering me. Aside from not hitting my head on a rock this time, this felt so familiar.

I remembered Jesse's arms wrapped around me, helping me back into my aunt's house. How safe I felt. My mind flipped through all the images of Jesse helping me during the week—even when I broke up with him, he still took care of returning the moped so I could catch the ferry. Helping me to leave him.

Suddenly, more than anything, I wanted to feel his arms around me.

I turned toward the car, trying to get a purchase so I could get up. The puddle was so cold. I was nose to nose with the back tire, which from this angle, I noticed was completely flat. I stood in the vacant dirt—mud—lot and yelled. Yelled for the flat tire, yelled for losing my aunt, yelled for Jesse losing his sister. Screamed into the driving rain and didn't care if I looked like a lunatic. I didn't want to go back to my apartment in Boston; all I wanted to do was see if Jesse was alright.

He had been there for me when I needed him—he had been everything I needed last week. And he was still grieving his sister's death In fact, my aunt's death had definitely brought everything back up. And yet, he had spent the week helping me. He had put me first. And I had taken him for granted.

I was definitely the most horrible person.

I shivered in my wet clothes, closed the trunk, and dragged my suitcase into the front seat with me. Hopefully, there was still something dry in there for me to put on.

First things first. I turned on the car and blasted the heat. Plugged in my almost-dead phone. Called triple-A. Let them know where I was and that I needed a tire changed.

Could I do it myself? Maybe. Did I want to stand in the rain and figure it out? No. I wanted out of these wet, muddy clothes. I opened up my suitcase. Most everything was damp. In the middle, I found a summer dress that I could throw on, along with a sweater.

I peeled off my muddy jeans, wet jacket, and wet shirt. Just then, the lights from the tow truck turned into the near-empty parking lot. Of course, when I was getting naked in my car, triple-A took no time at all. Any other time, they would take hours.

I shrugged on the dress and hoped the driver hadn't seen me in just my bra and panties. I shoved my feet back into the rain boots and my arms into the jacket. I grabbed the umbrella I kept under the car seat and hopped out to greet the triple-A person.

Stupidly, my sweater had still been on my lap, and it fell into a mud puddle. I shoved it back into my car and shivered in only my summer dress and my aunt's rain coat.

The triple-A guy was already examining the flat tire, keeping his eyes deliberately down. I was pretty sure he had seen something while I was changing.

"You have a spare?"

"In the trunk." Even though my face felt on fire and blushing, I was cold. My dress was way too light and the wind whipped up beneath it.

"I'll probably have to jack it up and since the ground is so soft right now, it would be dangerous for you to sit in the car while I do that. The car might slide off the jack. But you can sit in my truck—it's warm there—and wait."

"Really? Thank you so much." I popped the trunk for him, moved things around so he could access the spare, ran to the tow truck cab, and climbed in.

I leaned against the back of the seat and closed my eyes. Wishing for a nap. Dreading the drive to my apartment. It was only an hour and a half or two hours, nothing difficult. But I didn't want to go back. I didn't want to go back to any of it. My quiet life with few friends. My orderly apartment looking over city streets.

My apartment was just a place, and not a home at all. Other

than Cynthia and Sheila, I had let all my friends go. And even so, some of the friends I had met on the island already felt as close to me as my friends in real life. I thought it was because it was a vacation and I was just doing vacation things, but that wasn't what I had done all week on the island. I had done hard, real-life things. Sorted through my aunt's things, came to terms with her death, got closer to my mom and aunt, and had real fun going out with people on the island.

My fingers hit the button to call Cyn. If anyone could help me sort through my fragmented, tired thoughts, it would be her.

"Hey, Babe, how are you holding up?"

I burst into tears. When I could speak, I described what was happening: flat tire, couldn't get home.

"Well, is the Triple-A guy hot, at least?"

I giggled and that turned into a laughing-crying jag that must have concerned Cyn, because when she spoke again it was more serious than I had ever heard her voice.

"Babe, what's really going on?"

The words tumbled over each other, so fast I didn't know if I was being coherent. I told her all about Jesse. That I had never felt such a strong attraction to anyone ever before. Not when I started dating Frank, or Matt, or anyone.

And sure, I wasn't sure if Jesse's reaction to me was because of his sister's death, but I knew that *my* reaction was strong. But it was probably because I was dealing with my aunt's death.

And my family had finally mended. He was there for all that and I was mixing up all the feelings with him. Things had ended so poorly with Frank—in fact the whole Frank relationship was messed up.

And then I had dated Matt, and he had left, and I when I saw him again, those feelings were no longer there.

So how could I know that any feelings were permanent? How could I trust my heart? How could anyone know what was real? And then people leave and die. Maybe everyone was destined to be alone.

"You love him." Cyn broke into my rant.

The words shocked me. The cab of the truck was suddenly silent. Outside, the Triple-A guy started attaching my spare. Rain pelted him and the truck.

"Babe." Cyn's voice was calm and strong. "Trust yourself."

"Okay." An un-convinced, half question.

Then there was a long silence that gave me time to find peace. The peace I felt when I saw my mom and aunt reunite. The peace I felt when I saw all of my Aunt's friends in her backyard; a worthy goodbye. The peace when Sylvi told me how much the party meant to her.

The peace that made me feel that my aunt was still with me, still loving me, still championing me. The peace that peeled away all the anxious concerns I had about letting someone in. The peace that allowed me to feel the love I felt for my family, and my friends. And the peace that made me feel the strong, new, exciting love I felt for Jesse.

I loved Jesse.

"Okay," I repeated, but this time it wasn't a half-question. It was strong. It was knowing. It was me taking the trust Cyn had in me and using that to trust myself.

"I think I have to go back."

"What?" Cyn demanded as if she had heard the answer but needed to hear it again.

I remembered the feeling of not being able to leave Jesse without kissing him. I was not only drawn to the island. I was drawn to him. And he wasn't Frank. I could let myself fall for him if I wanted to.

Suddenly I very much wanted to. And of course, I had just broken things off with him. He very much could, and probably should, tell me that I didn't deserve a second chance. But I'd put myself out there anyway.

I cleared my throat. Rolled my shoulders back. "I have to go back."

"Yeah, you do. Call me later."

The triple-A guy climbed into the driver's seat and plugged a few things into his phone. "You should be all set; the new tire is on, the old one is in the trunk. Just replace that tire before you drive too long on the spare."

I wondered how much of my ranting he had heard and then I decided I didn't care. "Um, is there a better parking situation? I'm thinking of going back out to Stone's Throw Island."

"Sure is. There's long-term parking in a structure just on the other side of the ferry dock. You can leave your car there and it's cheaper than this lot. Plus, they rent spaces to island residents. I live part-time on the island and part-time on the mainland because my girlfriend lives in Providence. So, I keep my truck there a few days each week. Works out."

"Hmmm. It works out?"

"Hopefully it won't be like this forever, but for right now, it's the best of both worlds."

So, maybe there was an in-between.

I thanked the guy and climbed out of his truck and back into my car which was now steaming hot since I had left the heater running on high that whole time. I had a choice to make. Go back to my life in Boston, or explore what I found with Jesse.

I checked my watch. I had been off the ferry less than an hour and had plenty of time to catch the next one at three pm. If I wanted to do that.

And suddenly that's all I wanted to do. I plugged my phone back into the car charger and realized it wasn't holding the charge. It went blank, and I thanked the tech gods that my phone died *after* I called Triple-A.

No worries. I would just retrace my steps to the island. Rent a moped, get back to my aunt's house, take a shower, and somehow figure out how to get in touch with Jesse.

I pulled out of the parking lot and turned right to find the long-term lot. It was past the ferry dock and around the corner. The lot wanted me to pay by app, again, and my phone still wasn't charging. Probably due to landing in one too many puddles this week.

I could use my laptop to pay, but I'd need to find wi-fi first. I grabbed my laptop and suitcase and purse and locked the car, hoping I wouldn't get a second ticket while I was searching for a cafe with wi-fi.

The first cafe I stopped in had everything I was looking for. I ordered some coffee and a sandwich, pulled up the parking garage app, and paid for a week's parking. Done. Paid my parking ticket from the lot that gave me the flat tire. Done.

The booth I sat in was so comfy with heat that blasted down from a vent above me. I had thirty minutes before I needed to get back on the ferry. I could sit and wait here and finally warm up, or I could go out into the rain and find a new charger for my phone, assuming it was the charger and not the phone which was the issue. I decided I was a little too tired to wander back out into the rain. I'd just relax here until it was time to get back on the ferry. I didn't really need my phone, except to beg forgiveness from Jesse.

The warmth lulled my mind into a sleep-like state. Weariness washed over me. I couldn't risk missing the three pm ferry, so I ordered one more coffee, and hoped the caffeine would kick in. Finally, half asleep, I dragged my suitcase back out onto the ferry dock, stopped at the kiosk to buy a one-way ticket, and got in line.

The light dress under my Aunt's muddy raincoat wasn't the armor I wanted against the cold. I kept reassuring myself. In an hour, I'd be back on the island, fifteen minutes from then I'd be renting a moped, and fifteen minutes from then I'd be in my aunt's shower warming up. I could be cold for another hour and a half. I'd survive.

Behind me a heard a familiar voice.

"Paige! What are you doing?"

I turned to see Jesse striding up the pier to me, looking either determined or angry.

Or maybe both.

17

I whirled around. "Jesse? How did you get here?" Because that was the most important question. Not: Do you still want me? Which was the question I obviously wanted answered.

"Paige." He planted his feet in front of me like he was ready for a fight.

"I'm so sorry. I was wrong. I shouldn't have assumed your feelings for me weren't real. My feelings for you are real." I spoke candidly, probably because my mind was still in a tired, foggy haze. I didn't care that there was a small line of people, all a party to the speech that I hoped would get us back together.

"I'm sorry too. I didn't mean to suggest that you change your whole life for me. I can fit into your life too." He didn't seem to care that we were in public.

I wrapped my arms around him. "You were here for me all week. Thank you."

"You're freezing and your raincoat is completely wet. And a bit muddy."

"Mmm-hmm." I said into his jacket.

"Are you getting back on the ferry?"

"I don't know."

He held me at arm's length and looked at me like I was crazy. "You're in the ferry line, you know."

"I was ... coming to find you. Are you getting on the ferry?"

He smiled. "I am if you are."

"I am if you are." I repeated, stupidly.

"Do you have a ticket?"

"I got a one-way ticket."

"One-way, huh? I guess I should get one as well." He dropped out of line and I followed.

He texted on his phone all the way to the ticket kiosk. "I just had to let my friend know I don't need a ride back to the island, this evening when he returns. That I'm slumming it and taking the ferry." He bought his ticket and we walked back to the line.

My heart hummed. Fifteen minutes ago, I didn't know if he'd take me back. Fifteen minutes ago, I was on my own. I sighed.

Back in line, he pulled me to him. "You're really shivering. What on earth are you wearing?" He shook his head.

I tried to explain. "I fell in a mud puddle and had a flat tire and everything in my suitcase was wet except this dress. I had a sweater I was going to put on but then the tow truck guy drove up while I was mostly naked and I guess I forgot about it and when I got out the car, it fell in the mud ..."

"Half-naked, huh?" His grin was infectious. It was clear that he wanted half-naked in our future. I sighed again. This seemed too easy. I didn't have to fight to get him back; we just fell back together.

But then I realized that the story I just told him didn't seem easy. The decision to leave my life on the mainland wasn't easy. Getting things right with my family and my aunt hadn't been easy. I had taken charge and done the hard things.

Opening myself up to Jesse was my next hard thing. Allowing myself to grieve my aunt and help him live beyond his sister was the very next thing I wanted to do. And I knew it would be easier together. And that wasn't the coward's way out. It was the right way through.

We walked onto the ferry hand in hand. He carried my suitcase up the steps, stowed it in the luggage section, and steered me inside. I stopped at a booth with a table, but he directed me up a second, smaller staircase. At the top was the captain's cabin. He rapped on the door. A woman in a captain's hat opened it.

"Hey, Monique. Is the infirmary open? I need a blanket to warm up Paige. She's a magnet for hypothermia."

"Hey, I don't believe I've actually gotten hypothermia, thank you very much." I waved to Monique.

"Sure. I can give you the keys. Actually, if you wouldn't mind hanging in the infirmary for the whole trip, that would be excellent. We're short-handed today and the seas are rolling. Dramamine time." She held out her hand to me and added, "Nice to meet you, Paige. Enjoy the trip." Then she grabbed some keys hanging just inside the door and handed them to Jesse.

"Do you work for the ferry too?" Was there a job he didn't do?

"Sometimes I get called in when things are rough as a part of the emergency response team. I go where I'm needed." He led me down a short hallway.

"You're needed with me." I took his hand in mine. His was so warm. Safe. Strong.

He opened the last door on the corridor and pulled me into the infirmary just as the ferry horn blasted. It was tiny, with the traditional oval boat window on one wall, over an examination table covered with paper, with a curtain above it that could be pulled around for privacy. Cabinets lined the opposite wall.

"You came to the mainland for me!"

"I did. I returned the moped and was so angry you left without talking to me. And then I decided I didn't want that to stand. You weren't answering my texts. So I called around until I found someone coming to the mainland to pick up work supplies, and hitched a ride." He grabbed me around the waist and lifted me up on the table. "Take off that rain jacket."

I complied.

He opened and closed cabinets until he found a scratchy-looking blanket. "It's not soft, but it will keep you warm."

The boat moved beneath us, its engine vibrating the floor, the room dipping and rising in the swells.

Jesse opened up the blanket and pulled it behind me, easing himself between my legs until we were cuddled together, him leaning into me, me leaning into him, the blanket wrapped around both of us. He rubbed my arms and I started to feel warmer, safe, and happy.

I snuggled closer, pulling him to me. Warmth spread throughout my body. I leaned my forehead into his chest and he rested his chin on my head.

The swells of the boat pushed me into him, and I found the rhythm intoxicating. When the boat crested the waves, Jesse's body pressed me closer to the table. The next time a wave pushed me into him, I opened my legs as wide as they could go and Jesse moaned into my ear. There was one moment where a question was the only thing between us: would we?

And then Jesse pulled the curtain around the table. His hands found my butt and eased me farther back on the table, following me up and on his knees.

"Quiet, now," he whispered.

Oh my god, we were doing this.

"Jesse." Someone could walk in any minute.

"Paige." He pulled the dress off over my head and had my bra off in record time. I peeled his shirt off him, caressing his muscles and feeling the warmth and electricity roll through my body. Our mouths met and we kissed frantically as if we had been away from each other for years.

He pressed me down on the table, and the feeling of someone —anyone—walking in at any moment made me more assertive. The paper crinkled underneath us as I flipped us over and moaned into his ear. He pushed where I was growing wet, the rough fabric of his jeans softened by the cotton of my panties. The boat rocked us back and forth, and my muscles tightened, keeping me locked to him.

His tongue pushed deep into my mouth and I pushed my hips into him, as if I could push away the fabric between us. When I came up for air, I whispered fiercely in his ear, "Come inside me now."

Without moving my body from his, he unzipped his jeans, his knuckles rocking into my clit. I groaned. Loudly.

"Hush, Baby."

The puff of air from his words tickled my ears and his knuckles continued to massage inside me, through the cotton, and every bit of skin on my body pulsed with pleasure. I bit my lip to try to not exclaim.

"Jesse!" My plea was as quiet as I could make it. He pulled my underwear aside and plunged inside me with two fingers. I grabbed his cock in my hand, helped his free hand roll the condom on, and then massaged it while directing it inside me. He pulled his fingers out and plunged himself in deep. I gasped.

The rolling of the boat pushed us together harder than we could have on our own. Once, twice, three times, and I was trying to hold out from the orgasm. But I lost control. He flipped us over and timed his thrusts with the rolling of the waves. He saw my orgasm coming and held a hand gently over my mouth since I couldn't help but cry out.

The surge of the boat pushed him into me harder and farther than I thought possible. My body shuddered and I let go completely. He stayed there, pressed inside me, his weight on me, pressing all those parts inside me that made me respond. I let the waves inside me take me and lost all sense of where I was.

"Jesse," I breathed.

"Paige." He said like it was final.

★★★

Of course, I could have gotten off the ferry, re-rented my moped and got myself to Aunt Del's house. But it was so much nicer and warmer this way. Jesse grabbed my bag and hauled it down the steps and into his truck. He blasted the heater and drove me down the now-familiar lane to the beautiful weathered-shingle house. For the first time, I looked at it as if it wasn't just my aunt's house, but a little bit mine too.

On the way in, I grabbed the for-sale sign and pulled it out of the marshy grass. Dropped it flat against the porch. Until I made a firm decision, there was no need for it to be up.

Inside the house, I took off my aunt's jacket and hung it on the coat tree.

"Where do you want this?" Jesse held up my suitcase.

"Everything is wet inside it. I'm going to have to wash it all. I guess the laundry room?" I followed him in and grabbed my laptop from the bag. Threw most of the clothes directly into the washer and started it.

Jesse leaned against the door jam. "I have a few things I need to do today for work. You have everything you need?"

I didn't. The house, once again, was devoid of food and everyday items. But all that could wait. I wanted to take a shower, get into pajamas, and take a long nap. Then I could deal with all the work updates and look into what I could accomplish remotely. Work hadn't figured into my rash decision to come back to the island. But that was a question for later. "Maybe the number of a pizza place that delivers?"

"I'll tell you what. I'll stop by and grab some pizza on my way back from my work errands, tonight for a late dinner." He looked at his phone. "It's already four-thirty. I'll be back around seven, maybe." He grinned. "I don't expect this storm to be like the last one, but you never know. Don't try to pull any trees out of your windows this time, okay?"

He closed the distance between us and held my head in both hands, kissing me sweetly. I leaned in and wished he were staying. "I wish you were staying."

"My wish is that you stay here for good. Then we'd have all the time in the world."

I loved that. All the time in the world. I followed him out and shut the door behind him, suddenly feeling how thin and damp my sundress was on my skin. I turned the thermostat up and ran upstairs to get warmed up.

I ended up taking a long warm bath instead of a shower. I climbed into pjs and into bed, and woke up only when Jesse asked if he could join me. I opened up my arms and gathered him to me.

"Bells is so excited that you came back. I told her we could celebrate at Magnolia's tomorrow night. That's the only way she wouldn't barge over tonight."

"Mmmm. That's fine. Sounds good. Everything good on the island tonight?"

"You're here, so everything is more than good."

For the first time in a long time, I felt good, warm, safe.

I didn't even have to ask my Magic Eight Ball if all was right in my world. But if I did, I knew what it would say:

IT IS DECIDEDLY SO.

18

I woke up early and spent a few minutes lounging in bed, watching Jesse sleep. His face was relaxed and beautiful. When it started to feel like I was staring creepily, I gently moved out of bed, trying not to disturb the mattress or blankets.

I made coffee but again had no milk. No matter. The world outside was sunny and storm-washed. New-looking. That seemed to be the pattern here. Stormy then beautiful. Just like life. Sometimes rain and hardship fell and then the world was new again. The newness didn't take away from the sadness and grief. It just added some happiness.

Birds tweeted outside. I grabbed the outside furniture out of the shed again and one by one carried them back out to the back deck. Finally settled, I sat with a second cup of coffee and enjoyed the morning.

Before long, Jesse came down, and I grabbed him a black cup of coffee as well. We sat together in silence.

"I spent many days out here with your aunt and my sister. Do you mind if I talk about her?"

And for the first time, I didn't feel that talking about his sister and his connection to this house and my aunt took anything away from our own relationship.

"Talk away." I wanted to try out my theory that we could work through our losses together, and that it didn't have to be one person being strong and putting themselves aside for the other. That we could both be weak and vulnerable together and that would make the difference.

"Your aunt would hand her binoculars and they would name all the different types of birds that flew in and out of the backyard and bog." We watched the swooping birds in silence for a few moments.

"I couldn't believe how long they could stay, intently watching the smallest animals going about their day and find it so fascinating. It made me realize that these moments, these small moments, are when life is real. My work is about saving and fixing and building and all these huge gestures. But life isn't always like that. Being peaceful in the small moments matters."

That reminded me of Jack and the ferry ride over that felt like a lifetime ago.

"Being present in those moments is magic." I looked off the porch and tried to imagine my aunt here with his sister. I had gone on walks and bike rides with my aunt, her binoculars dangling from her neck, and she had pointed out egrets and seagulls and smaller birds I didn't remember. I had always wanted to see a hummingbird and she said I had to be patient and be still.

"Let's get a hummingbird feeder and hang it off the deck."

"Let's."

"Paige!" Bells' voice echoed through the mostly empty house.

Jesse smiled. "Told you I couldn't keep her away."

"Out here!"

"Oh my gosh, you guys look so cute." Bells walked through the open slider and put a box from the cafe on the table. "I thought you'd need food. Penny is very excited you're staying."

Jesse opened the box. "Penny must be extremely happy—this

is filled with her greatest hits. Cream-cheese waffle bites. Baby cinna-buns. Apple cider donut holes."

"Are you coming in today to the general store, Jesse?"

"My shift starts at ten, so I'm leaving in thirty or so. Paige, I can drop you off at the moped rental place before work so you can get around today."

"I have to figure out my work if I'm staying. So, I'll be good here for the day. I have the bike if I need anything. It's a beautiful day, no worries about me getting around."

"I don't want to leave you stranded. Especially since your phone isn't working."

"Don't worry, I'll be fine even if I can't get my phone to turn on. I just want a quiet, do-nothing day. I'll take a look at it now." I kissed him gently and he and Bells dug into the pastries on the porch.

I checked to see if my phone was holding a charge. Maybe I should have put it in rice last night. Not that I had rice. I added that to the mental list I started when I woke up. Milk. Eggs. Rice for my phone.

It didn't look good. The phone face was black, without that reassuring plugged-in-and-charging icon that it normally would have if it was working. I could text people from my laptop so my family knew where I was and wouldn't worry, but I definitely needed to get a new phone delivered. I doubted there was a phone store on the island, but who knew? This island continued to surprise me.

I wandered around the house and looked at it with fresh eyes. It was almost empty of all my aunt's things except for the furniture. I didn't know what the future held for me, but I was thinking I'd keep it. Maybe rent it out the weeks I needed to be in Boston for work. Or not. The idea of strangers using what more and more felt like my own house, didn't sit right with me.

I straightened a picture of the sunset over the northern lighthouse in the library and wondered what the dark shelves would look like holding all my books. I was already moving in, in my mind. I smiled. What a difference a week could make in a life. In a family.

I went upstairs, grabbed my laptop from the bedroom, and plugged it in in the office. It would be easy to do most of my work remotely. Of course, the marketing firm I was a part of might disagree. But maybe clients would enjoy an escape to an island for a meeting. A part of the charm of working with me.

I settled into the chair, opened up my laptop and started answering emails and organizing the work I had put aside for the last week. I heard Jesse start the shower upstairs. Bells stopped in to let me know she was leaving and to make sure I knew that she expected me at Magnolia's that night at seven-thirty. "We're going to celebrate you not leaving the island. Maybe get you to move over for good!"

I stood and gave her a long hug. "Thank you."

"You're welcome, but for what?"

"Just for being a friend. For being you."

"That's weird. Who else would I be? I'll see you at seven-thirty."

I continued to answer the millions of emails I had ignored all week until Jesse came down the stairs and hovered in the doorway.

"I have to go to work. You going to be okay?"

I stood and stretched. "I'm great. Looking forward to a peaceful day. Figure out where I am work-wise and just relax."

"You look good here."

"In my aunt's study?"

"Here, in my life. On the island. In *your* study."

"I guess it is mine. But still my aunt's, you know?"

"It will always be Delilah's; you wouldn't be here if it wasn't for her, but sometimes legacy is the best way to find your own home."

I wondered if Jesse was thinking just of my aunt's house and how I was making it my home for the time being, or whether he was also thinking of his sister's house. I wondered what would happen to that house; her legacy.

I kissed Jesse deeply—another goodbye kiss—but so unlike the kiss from the day before at the ferry dock. This one promised a beginning instead of an end.

I spent the day just feeling good in my skin, on the island, in the house. Making things mine in a way I had never done before. Instead of wondering what I *should* do or be, I thought of what I *wanted* to do and who I *wanted* to be.

I biked into town at lunchtime and to see Penny and thank her for the delicious breakfast. She finally let me pay for my lunch and let me try some pancake recipes she wasn't selling yet. Delicious.

I spent the rest of the afternoon poking through the open stores in town. Many businesses were still closed until the true start of the season—Memorial Day weekend—but I did find a clothing store off the beaten path that was open and bought a sparkly top. I'd use it to dress up my jeans for the evening out. I happily biked back home, showered again, put on makeup and my new top, enjoying taking the time to breathe. To not rush getting ready for the night. I was fully relaxed by the time Jesse arrived with pizza.

I met him at the door. "I'm thinking of getting a pet," I announced.

He beamed at me. "You really are moving in, aren't you?"

"I guess I don't really do anything half-assed."

He put the pizza on the kitchen counter and pulled me to him, grabbing my butt. "Definitely not half-assed."

"Hey!"

"Totally a compliment." He nuzzled me in his arms. "Thank you."

"For what?"

"For giving 'us' a chance." He kissed me deep and slow. And then pulled away to open the pizza box. "But we're already late and Bells has been texting me repeatedly." We stood in the kitchen and ate the pizza standing up. I checked my phone plugged in on the counter; still dead. I held it up for Jesse to see.

"That's okay, I don't plan on letting you out of my sight tonight."

Jesse's phone buzzed and buzzed. "How do you feel about eating on the way? Bells is going to have my head if I don't get you to the bar asap."

"Sounds fine to me." I finished my slice and grabbed another. I was starving after biking in the island air.

We piled into the truck and he told me about the renovations he was finishing up at one of the island's bed and breakfasts. He was happy they'd be done before the tourist season started.

We were at the bar before I was even finished with my pizza so we sat and watched the last ferry of the day arrive at the pier. People filed off and went their ways. Jesse talked of all the parts of the island I still needed to see, that he wanted to show to me.

"You ready?" Jesse seemed more relaxed than I had ever seen him. I loved it.

"Ready." I climbed out of the truck and Jesse was already there, to grab my hand. The lights turned on around us, and again I thought how magical the strip of town looked.

★★★

If the party in my backyard was for Aunt Del, this gathering at the bar felt like a party for me.

First off, as I walked in, Bells yelled, "Paige!" and everyone turned to us. I blushed at the attention but pumped my hand in the air. Bells' energy was infectious. Jesse held onto my waist, possessively, as we hurried to the table our Nellie and Drew were holding.

I added an extra sashay to my steps, grinning widely, bumping my hips into Jesse. He grabbed a seat and pulled me onto his lap, to my protest. "Jesse, we're in public!"

He held on tight and wouldn't let me go. He whispered into

my ear and his warm breath shot tingles into my core. "I'm counting down the seconds until we're by ourselves."

The waitress delivered a tray of drinks, and I snuggled into Jesse, feeling warm, safe, and happy. So happy. And totally aroused. I drank my Dark 'N' Stormy in a couple of gulps, happy to be here, but also looking forward to being alone with Jesse. Everything was good.

I let the conversation float over me while I just was.

Jesse's phone buzzed underneath me and I wiggled around to let him get to it. He whispered in my ear, "When I have you to myself, we're going to do this, naked." I wiggled around a little more, and he groaned into my ear, before answering the phone.

"Hello?"

I could hear my mom's voice over the phone. She sounded concerned and I realized I hadn't let her know that my phone was dead. I had meant to, but I hadn't even checked my texts on my computer.

"She's great, and right here." Jesse passed the phone to me.

"Hey, mom! I'm so sorry, my phone died in the rain. Like, permanently died."

"I'm so relieved." My mom's voice was barely comprehendible over the jukebox and bar noises. The bar was raging tonight.

"Mom, I'm going to go outside, so I can hear you better. Give me a minute."

I got up and Jesse stood too. I waved him off. He looked concerned and then held out the keys to his truck.

"At least sit in comfort while you talk. It's a little chilly out there."

I nodded, took the keys, and continued with my mom. "I have some news, but I'll tell you when I can hear you better."

I quickly exited Magnolia's and shivered in the blast of spring nighttime air.

All the pretty fairy lights were on and I felt the magic of it all. The friends, Jesse; the island itself. I was pretty sure my mom wouldn't be surprised to hear I was moving here permanently.

"So, Mom, I don't think I'm going to sell Aunt Del's house." I hiked up into the cab of Jesse's truck.

"That's wonderful, Paige. Are you going to rent it out?"

I settled into the truck and turned it on, blasting the heat.

"Um, no, I kinda want to—"

The passenger door opened and I screamed a little bit, out of surprise.

"Paige?!" My mom yelled into the phone.

Frank hopped up beside me.

"What on earth are you doing here? Mom, it's okay, it's just—"

"Paige." Frank's voice was guttural and controlling.

And that's when I saw the gun in his hand.

"Give me the phone."

Instead, I grabbed the door handle and pushed it. Frank grabbed my arm, keeping me in the cab, and I squealed. The phone fell to my lap, my mom's yelling voice far away. Frank kept my arm in an iron grip and put the gun carefully on his lap, grabbed the phone, and threw it out the window.

He reached across me, closed my door, and I could smell alcohol on his breath.

Okay, he was drunk, had a gun, and was hurting my arm. But I knew this man, we had been together a while. I could talk to him and this would be okay.

It would be okay, right?

I didn't have an answer and all I could imagine the Magic Eight Ball responding was with:

ASK AGAIN LATER.

19

I looked to Magnolia's door and willed someone to come out. And then shook my head. No. I didn't want anyone else involved. In fact, while I was sure that Frank wouldn't do anything to me, I wasn't sure that he wouldn't hurt someone else. How much time would elapse before Jesse felt like checking on me? Jesse. I couldn't risk that Frank wouldn't hurt Jesse.

"Drive." Frank picked up the gun and dug it into my side. I remembered that dark night that I was held up at gunpoint with my brother, my friends, and Matt, the night my brother proposed to Jinx, and another wave of fear washed over me.

I put the truck in gear and gave a moment of thanks that I was driving Frank with the gun away from Bells. Away from Margo, Nellie, Drew, and everyone in the bar. Away from Jesse. Far away from Jesse. I had to keep him safe. No matter that all the self-defense courses taught me to never ever go to a second location with someone threatening. Nothing good ever happened at a second location. I shivered, even though the heat was still blasting in the cab.

We drove down the main strip and when Frank growled,

"Keep straight." I stayed straight at the circle at the end. We drove past cliffs on one side and an alpaca farm on the right.

"Where are we—"

"Shut up."

I shut up. Things were still fine. Really. I could negotiate with Frank as soon as we got far away from the bar and the people I had grown to love.

Fog rolled over the car and I couldn't tell if the mist on the windshield was from rain, or just water off the ocean. The cab grew claustrophobically hot and I turned off the heat and put on the defroster.

"Frank." I tried again.

"If I can't have you then nobody can."

Oh. My. God. My understanding of the situation jack-knifed and I suddenly knew things were not going to be okay. Frank was going to kill me. And I didn't even get to say goodbye to my mom. That asshole had thrown the phone from the truck. I didn't get to explore my relationship with Jesse. My friendship with Bells. My new island home. Anger flooded to the surface. Who did he think he was, deciding when MY life ended?

I turned to give him a fucking piece of my mind, but when he saw the look on my face, he pushed the gun into my side harder and commanded, "Pull over here."

We were at the overlook at Hilde's Hollow. A cliff, with a treacherous number of steel steps, winding down the straight drop to the beach below. If that's where we were headed, then maybe I could somehow wrestle the gun from Frank on the way down. *Please give me the time to figure this out.* I prayed into the stifling heat of the cab.

Frank pulled me across the cab, and out his door, the truck still running, the lights still on, which I was thankful for. At least the night wasn't completely black. I wasn't thankful for the bruised arm where Frank kept ahold of me, the bruised side where the gun pressed, or the scrapes and bumps from being hauled out of the truck.

The waves crashed way below us, and Frank pulled me to the steps, dangerous in the daytime when I could hold on to both handrails, ridiculously dangerous in the dark of the night. He held onto the gun and the guardrail with one hand, me in the other; the gun clanked eerily against the metal of the railing with each step.

I shivered violently in the cold air, my feet sliding on the slick metal stairs, trying to stay upright while Frank pulled me forward. A few of the top steps were lit by the truck's headlights, but the light was trapped in the fog and after the first ten steps, yes, I was counting, darkness engulfed me. I considered using my weight to push us into a free-fall, but that seemed even more dangerous than the gun.

Maybe I could still get out alive. This was Frank. I had loved him for a year before things had gone south. But this wasn't the Frank I knew. That Frank had been never angry. This Frank, I didn't recognize at all.

I lost my footing and his grasp on me tightened to keep me on the steps, dragging me behind him. I hit the side railing hard and grabbed it.

"Can we stop? I'm ..."

"Shut up."

I stumbled down; certain I was going to topple us down the steps. No way we could stay upright at this pace. "Frank."

"I said, 'Shut up.'"

"We're going to fall."

He seemed to come to his senses and slowed a little, so I could catch myself on the railing and feel the next step below with my foot.

A little more in control, I tried to think.

I had left him. Then his mom died. So, he didn't have anyone left. No, he didn't have any *family* left. Even when he was screwing around on me with other women, he still wanted me to be his family; he had proposed to me when he thought he lost me.

I was thinking so hard I lost count and stumbled down a step, hitting Frank's back hard with my whole self. For a moment, I thought we were goners, and then he pushed me back into the guardrail with such force that I lost my breath.

"Watch it."

Once I could take a breath again, "It's dark. Let's slow down. Let's talk."

"What do we have to talk about?"

"Do you want to—you know—get back together?" It was all I could think to say that might save my life.

"Shut up, shut up, SHUT UP."

He pulled me down to a landing and faced me. Pressed the gun into my side. "The time for that was before. Before you rejected my ring. Threw it across the floor. Before you flaunted your new guy in front of me. Before you threw me away like *garbage.*"

With each sentence, he pressed the gun deeper into my stomach. I couldn't move and everything I said to him seemed to set him off.

He turned and started back down the stairs. Mumbling more to himself than me. "Wasn't there when Mom died. Pretended to be there when I got to the island but it was all just FAKE. Pretending to care. Pretending what we had mattered."

I held tight to the railing and tried to keep up with him so he didn't pull me along. I didn't think it a good idea to remind him he had cheated on me—that he had forgotten what mattered. Or maybe he thought that he could cheat on someone and still have them. My anger flared and heated me. Who was he to control me? I had thrown him out of my life; who was he to come back into it?

My feet hit sand and I lost my footing and stumbled, yet I had never felt anything so welcoming in my life. No longer afraid of falling to my death, I recognized that I had nothing else to lose—all my friends and Jesse were safe. I gave in to the anger.

"You threw what we had away, Frank. That was you."

He let go of me and backed off a foot or so. The moon came out behind clouds and gave me a clear view of my ex.

He stood, feet wide apart, and pulled the gun up so it was aimed directly at my chest.

"You would talk to me like that while I'm holding a gun on you?"

I shrugged, trying to hide the fact that my heart was racing so badly I wondered if it could burst. "What do I have to lose?"

He grinned. "Nothing. You're mine now."

The grin made me even angrier. "You cheated on me. And you think you still deserve me?"

He shrugged, eerily calm in the moonlight. "You were always mine; you just didn't always know it. Now, do you know it?"

The chill running down my spine had nothing to do with the cold wind whipping around us. My mind went into calculations that I seemed to have no control over. To my right was a cliff face. Behind me were the stairs and more cliffs. To my left was the ocean, almost too peaceful in its constant motion. All the warnings of the cold water, of the dangers of hypothermia, filled my head.

Every single direction spelled death, but the number one death was my ex with a gun. I couldn't make it up the stairs without him killing me. If I ran to the ocean, well, at least maybe I could control my death. This asshole wouldn't control me, and denying him that seemed the last power I had. I'd choose the cold water. I'd choose hypothermia.

But it was still ten feet or so to the water. I didn't know what kind of shot Frank was. Where had he even gotten that gun? *Focus, Paige.* If I ran for the water, I didn't want him to hit me. I wanted him to know that he was ineffectual in his final act. That I would die on my own terms. I braced myself in the sand and tried to figure out how to distract him.

"I was never yours. You can't own someone, Frank. No matter how much you want to. Do you hear me? Never *yours.*"

I was so focused on making myself pick a moment to run into the frigid water, that whatever happened above and behind me was lost to me. All I knew was Frank took his eyes off me for a second, and like a sprinter hearing the starting gun, I blasted toward the water. Zig-zagging.

Hitting the surf and trying to get under those black waves. I dove in and when I came up, not able to catch my breath, I heard shots. Dove back under. Pain hit every part of my body, the cold unbearable. I flipped over and tried to breathe, but my lungs wouldn't pull in. I tried not to splash, tried to ignore the pain, tried to lie beyond the wave break, hoping that since I couldn't see him, Frank couldn't see me.

I just couldn't catch my breath. My body started going numb. I turned my eyes to the beach and realized I could see Frank looking at the waves, but not at me. He had lost track of me. Would he come into the water after me? I didn't think it would matter.

I pulled in a shallow breath and tried to calm myself. If I couldn't catch my breath, there would be no hope. Frank wasn't my concern anymore—panic and hypothermia were. I welcomed a weird warmth into my hands and feet.

I must have been imagining things. I saw spots of light on the beach. Circles of light. Like flashlights. And then Frank was no longer standing there, Jesse was.

I closed my eyes. Clearly my mind was playing tricks on me. That was still Frank with a gun. I ducked under the wave and into the frigid, dark water. Keeping my feet up from the nipping crabs in the sand. I needed to stay hidden and just take one damn breath.

I came up out of the wave and my eyes found Jesse, running into the water. He was closer now and I somehow knew it wasn't a trick of my mind. It was him. And I knew he was too late. My limbs felt too heavy to keep above the surface, and I just couldn't pull in enough air. Lightheaded and warm, I sank back into the water, letting it cradled me. The moon disappeared and darkness, soft, warm, blackness was all that there was.

20

Something grabbed me out from the warm embrace of the ocean. Something hard and unforgiving. I broke the surface and pain shot through every cell of my body.

"C'mon, babe, breathe. I got you."

"Hot. Cold. Hurts." Hot pokers stabbed my hands and feet. "Jesse?"

"I'm here. We gotta get you warm. It'll be okay. It'll be okay." But his voice was panicked.

"Oh my god, you got her!" Bells' voice came from nowhere.

"Not out of the woods, yet."

Sirens rang out and suddenly I was bouncing up the steps, banging hard into Jesse. I kept my eyes closed against the pain and tried to find a soft spot to rest against. "Stop? Please?"

"I'm so sorry. But I have to get you warm. Just ... I'm sorry."

The pounding and bouncing got worse.

"Bells has the perp. Is the ambulance here?"

Some gruff voice I'd never heard before said, "On its way." I enjoyed the respite from the banging while that short conversation ran its course.

I tried to get back that feeling of safety and security that I had always felt in his arms. But all I felt was pain. "Hurts."

"I know darling, but the quicker we get to the truck, the quicker you warm up."

I considered this answer and how the steps went on forever.

Finally, we were up at the top and back to his truck, which blissfully was still running. He climbed with me into the driver's side and turned sideways so he was still holding me, blasting the heat on us both. New feelings of pain shot into fingers and toes that I hadn't felt in a while. I moaned.

"That's good, babe. Pain is good. It means things are alive. Shit. You're alive." He vigorously rubbed my fingers. Which hurt like hell. But all I could do is lean against him and moan.

We stayed like that for what felt like forever, the pain shooting through my body and me wishing for it all to just stop. Then he reached behind the seat and pulled out a blanket, scratchy as hell, pulled off my wet shirt, pulled off his wet shirt, and wrapped that blanket around our bodies. I just grunted.

"So, I have this problem."

I leaned into his warmth, for a moment feeling less pain and safer, and said, "Mmh-hmm?"

Blinking red lights interrupted him, so bright I could see them with my eyes closed—red splashes against the darkness.

He shifted. "I don't want to let you go."

The heat lulled me and the pain was receding and all I could say was, "I'm not going anywhere, ever." Then sleep, or at least unconsciousness, crashed in.

★★★

The hospital released me in the morning, my medical team reassuring me I'd keep every single finger and toe. Telling me not to go swimming in the ocean in the spring. Then a wink or a nod, telling me, without telling me, that they knew exactly what happened. All of the nurses and doctors who cared for me thanked me for the party at Aunt Del's house. Either everyone in the whole hospital knew and loved Aunt

Del, or these doctors had each requested to be at my bedside.

Jesse never left me. He was dressed in scrubs, since his clothes had gotten soaked when he dove into the ocean to save me. When I asked, he told me that he had gone looking for me not too long after I left. He had found the phone broken on the road and his truck gone. He and Bells had jumped onto borrowed mopeds, lent for the chase, and Jesse had gone in one direction while Bells went the other. Soon he had found his truck and the rest was what I remembered: him saving me from the cold ocean.

He bundled me into his truck, tucking a hospital blanket around me.

"I am not a china doll." But the blanket was nice and warm and I didn't have a jacket against the morning chill. The sun was hidden behind gray clouds and it looked a little like a storm was rolling in.

The truck glided slowly out of the parking lot as if any bump might shatter me. I thought about saying something and then decided his concern was nice. I settled back into the truck, feeling safe and finally relaxed.

"You can turn off the heat now. It's oven-hot in here." I snuggled closer into his side and pulled the blanket up around my shoulder, wanting its comfort even as I complained about how hot the cab had gotten.

Jesse turned the heat down and pulled the edge of the blanket up to my ears. "Whatever you want, babe."

With Jesse driving like an old lady, the ride from the hospital to my aunt's house—no, my house—took forever. And I wondered why he didn't bring up what I had said last night—that I was never going anywhere again.

I guessed I was the one who was going to have to bring it up, here in this truck on an island that didn't allow trucks, with this man, who had literally saved my life.

"I've decided to stay."

"Okay."

That wasn't the response I had anticipated. Maybe fireworks and a parade? But not a simple, "okay."

"What do you mean, 'Okay?'"

He snuck his arm under the blanket and around me. "I mean, okay."

I sat up and pulled away from his arm, keeping the cozy blanket around me. "I just told you I was moving my ENTIRE life onto a tiny island WHICH KEEPS TRYING TO KILL ME, and all you can say is, 'Okay?' Are you serious?"

He chuckled, which infuriated me even more. "Babe, if you want fanfare, there's some waiting at your house."

I pondered that and snuggled back into him, still a little mad. I could cuddle and be mad at the same time. He was just so nonchalant and infuriating about my life-changing news. I was moving to the island for him. And the island did keep trying to kill me.

"The island wants me dead." I knew I was acting like a child. But since I had almost died last night, I could be forgiven, I thought.

He finally pulled up to my house, and pulled me even closer to him, holding me in his lap. "The island doesn't care one way or another who lives or dies. You just keep making stupid decisions." His voice was all calm and deep, and it sounded lovely, what he said, until I thought about the actual words.

"I don't keep making stupid decisions." My words would have had more impact if they weren't muffled by his shoulder. But I wasn't ready to let go of him, even if we were going to have a fight. In fact, this was the perfect place for a fight.

"You do, babe. You sure do."

"Trying to pull a tree out of my window is stupid?!"

"Yup. Dangerous. As you experienced."

"Then what, do YOU think, I should have done?"

He shrugged, which moved my head up and down. "Called the Emergency Response Crew, of course." Lightning zigged across the sky in the distance. "Let's go in before it starts to rain."

I nodded but moved slowly like I was in a dream. The toll from the night still weighed on my body. He was out of the car and opening my door before I could even shift my weight to my side of the cab. He gently eased me across the seat, so careful of the bruises Frank had inflicted last night. Like he had memorized where they were on my body. I sighed.

"And last night? Jumping into the ocean saved me. Kinda."

"Yeah, your midnight swim that almost killed you? Definitely a bad idea. But that wasn't your stupid decision. Your stupid decision was leaving the bar with that asshole."

I cuddled into his body and let him carry me up the steps to the house. "I couldn't let him and his gun anywhere near you. Or Bells."

He stopped suddenly. The door swung open to the house, and Bells stood in the doorway as if she had been conjured up by my words, or maybe the storm winds that were suddenly swirling around us. Jesse pulled me tight to him and whispered fiercely in my ear, "You never confront danger without me. Promise me. Now."

"Or me!" Bells hugged me and Jesse. "Remember, I run toward danger!" She released us quickly and tried to usher us into the house. "A storm is coming."

"Bells." His voice was a low warning. But he was looking at me. He gently put me down on the porch and held my face in his hands. "Promise me. We tackle danger together."

"I promise." And that promise rewarded me with the best kiss of my life.

Without a doubt.

21

Jesse, Bells, and I sat in the kitchen nook and watched, through a perfect picture window, the storm roll in over the ocean, over the bog, and into the backyard.

"Let's let Paige rest. Last night was a lot." Jesse pulled my hand into both of his.

"You mean, 'Bells, get out of here, so I can get my groove on with Paige.'"

"No. I mean, let's let Paige rest and recuperate."

"Sure, in a bit." Bells checked her giant sports watch and then her phone. "A few more minutes." I didn't know what was going on, but clearly something, since Jesse gave in without any more of a fight.

Lightning raced across the sky and thunder boomed. My attention shifted from my shifty friend and boyfriend and out into the now-dark afternoon.

You'd think I'd feel anxiety watching the storm after all the things that had happened during the first storm, but Bells' excitement was infectious. Plus, Jesse had a way to make me feel more than safe. I held on to his hand and studied his face. He smiled back at me.

"There's *nothing* like a good storm." Bells stood and leaned toward the bay window as if she needed to be closer to outside to get a good look.

I grinned while Jesse rolled his eyes. "Don't teach Paige bad habits about storms. I'm trying to keep her safe, and that's no easy task."

And that's when I realized how quickly and completely my life had irreparably changed. That man on the ferry, Jack, had been exactly right. The island was magic. Well, maybe not just the island. Maybe there had always been magic in life, and the island had just helped me to notice it. Which seemed like something Jack would say, too.

A knock sounded on the front door and as if my thoughts had conjured him up, Jack walked in with a cheery, "Hello, folks!" Scrambling around him was an adorable black puppy on a leash, and I dropped out of the chairs and onto the floor to accept squirrelly puppy kisses.

"Gramps, you made it!" Bells called out, falling to her knees beside me.

"Gramps?"

"Jack is my grandfather. He loves you, by the way."

Jack nodded his head. "The party for Del was perfect. Thank you for that, darling."

I stood to be folded into Jack's arms as if he was *my* grandfather.

That's when I noticed a small pet carrier on the counter, way too small for the puppy on the floor. What was inside? Did Jack travel everywhere with his pets?

The puppy jumped around my legs, and I extricated myself from Bells' grandfather to pick him up. "You have the cutest puppy, Jack."

But it was Jesse who spoke. "*You* have the cutest puppy, Paige." Jesse came up behind me and pulled me into his arms.

"He's for me?" I craned my neck to smile at him. But then the puppy squirmed and got all my attention again.

Jesse kissed the top of my head. "She's for you. Well, really, she's for me. With a little luck, she'll grow to be a good watchdog. With her with you, you'll always have some protection, even when I'm not around."

Normally, I would have argued that I could handle myself, but after last night's events, I would take all the protection I could get. Plus, the puppy was *so* cute.

I held onto the squirming ball of black and nestled us into Jesse's arms.

"Check out her name." Jesse turned over the silver heart on her polka-dot collar and I read, Puddle.

"Puddle?"

"Where I first saw you, in that puddle. And then you stood up, sparks in your eyes and on your tongue, and I knew I had to know you."

I narrowed my eyes, reliving that moment when I landed in cold water because I was surprised by Jesse's truck. But it was impossible for me to stay even mock-mad with a puppy licking my face.

"Thank you! Puddle is perfect."

Bells pointed to the pet carrier. "My gift is there."

She bounced over, unzipped the door, and scooped out a beautiful mewing torti-colored kitten. "My gift isn't as self-centered as Jesse's is. This is just for you, no strings attached."

"You remembered I said I was thinking of getting a cat!"

"Of course. Although I was self-centered enough to name her as well. Crash."

Jack chuckled.

"Crash is perfect for a kitten!" I handed Puddle to Jesse and cuddled Crash to my cheek. She stopped mewing to purr.

"Well, also because if it wasn't for a tree crashing through your window, none of the week might have happened. You might have just sold your aunt's house and went back to your life on the mainland."

Clearly, Bells had thought about this. "I'm grateful that the storm made you meet us and stay. And now, really stay. Consider

Crash a house warming gift and a reminder that storms are amazing things that can change your life."

Suddenly I could see the resemblance between Jack and Bells, not just in features, but in perspective. And for the first time in forever, I felt at content, safe, and just where I was supposed to be.

But also tired. So very tired.

Jesse studied my face, like he had been watching for the sleepiness to creep in.

"Alright, you two, thanks for the delivery. I'm going to make sure Paige sleeps. There will be all the time in the world after she officially moves here. Out."

"Keys, please." Bells held out her hand.

"Xavier dropped me off, so I wouldn't have to wrestle a cat and a dog on my bike," Jack explained to me.

Jesse tossed his truck's keys to Bells and ushered the two to the front door. I trailed behind, with a sleeping kitten in my hand. I wasn't too far behind Crash in wanting to get to sleep.

After he shut the door, without a word, he led me upstairs and into the bedroom. It felt like we had done this for years, and would do it for years to come. We settled into the bed, with kitten by my side, a puppy on his, holding each other as the storm raged outside.

★★★

Want more Stone's Throw Island romances? Get exclusive stories in your in box by signing up at: www.stonesthrowisland.com

Keep reading for a sneak peek of Xavier and Violet's story in Samantha Mayson's Stone's Throw Island romance, A SEA OF CHANCES.

(Keep an eye out for Bells' epic Stones' Throw Island romance! Coming out in 2023)

A SEA OF CHANCES

VIOLET AND XAVIER'S STORY BY SAMANTHA MAYSON

Stepping off the ferry, the smells hit me first. Stone's Throw Island has that mixture of sea, salt and fried fish that brought me back to another time. Laura and her three Tri Delta sisters "woo-wooed" as they strutted down the ramp and hit the concrete dock. I kept renaming the Three Ashleys (all spelled differently, I learned from the email exchanges planning this trip), in my mind to Muffy, Buffy and Mittsy, but I knew that wasn't fair of me. They were Laura's friends from college and we were here for her bachelorette weekend. They hated me because I was the maid of honor and I hated them because ... well, they existed.

I was not thrilled with Laura's choice in weekend getaways, just as much as I wasn't thrilled with her choice in grooms, but I always took care of my baby sister and I was determined to make sure she had the time of her life.

I flagged down one of the locals who waited by the ferry with their truck, something I saw my dad do every summer growing up. I had no idea what to pay or tip them, and my budget for this weekend was very limited, but I gave him the address of the cottage we rented for the weekend (thank goodness it was still officially off-season) and he delivered our bags for us.

"I hope we can trust that guy," said Ashley, or was it, Ashleigh?

"No worries, the people here *live* for the tourists, they wouldn't screw it up," my sister responded. Her tone was full of entitlement and not like someone who grew up straddling the line between tourist and local.

My dad had grown up on the island. His family owned a small house near the center bog of the island, and we spent every summer here. Dad would go back and forth to the mainland for work, but Mom, Laura, and I would stay all summer with Nanny. We knew the locals and they accepted us as one of them. I even worked at Oceanside Cafe our last summer here.

"First, we have to rent bikes," Laura was commanding. "It's the only way to get around the island. Violet, lead the way."

Muffy, Tuffy and Cottontail looked like they would rather ride the Green Line then get on a bike and I couldn't blame them. Their short skirts were not conducive to biking, nor riding a ferry or dealing with the rustic roads of Stone's Throw Island. They were probably expecting something glamorous, with yachts and mansions and champagne fountains.

I really need to stop calling them names like that.

I led the way to the bike/moped rental shop that was across from the ferry. Even though it was only May, it was a nice weekend and there were bikes parked outside. Just before we went in, I glanced down the road. I knew the Oceanside Cafe was still open, I mean, Google exists, but the site was probably last updated when I worked there ten years ago. I wondered if *he* was still working there.

Lauren, who was only fourteen the last summer we spent on Stone's Throw, knew about Xavier, but she didn't know everything. I couldn't believe it when she told me this is where she wanted to have her bachelorette weekend. She got to go to college in Boston and I was sure she'd want to stay at some fancy hotel and go to a dance club near Faneuil Hall or something, but she was adamant about this. "That way, it's girls only, no interruptions from the guys." The guys being Chris, her fiancé and his frat brothers, the male equivalent of The Ashleys.

The thing about The Ashleys is they all look the same. They all have the exact same balayaged wavy hair, as if they each saw the same stylist and said, "I'll have what she's having." At least Lauren knew better than to try dying her dark brown hair, but she had the same perfect waves. My hair hadn't been treated in a salon since my prom night. After years of cutting it myself, my hair was natural, a little frizzy, and always worn in a ponytail. The girls complained about the wind on the ferry ride over here, but I didn't worry about getting hair in my mouth.

I'm nothing if not practical.

After renting bikes, Lauren declared that she was famished and we just *had* to go to the Oceanside Cafe because, "they have THE BEST pancakes! and THE MUFFINS! It's worth the calories, Girls!" It was true, they did, but I wished she would have given me a chance to ... I don't know. Get ready? Clean up?

"Maybe we should go check in first?" I asked.

"No way, I'm starved, and I can smell Penny's muffins from here. C'mon!"

I reminded myself that this was Lauren's weekend, and reluctantly followed. Because, possibly, in that cafe was the first (and if I'm being honest, only) love of my life, Xavier Bennet.

Xavier's parents owned the Oceanside and they lived on Stone's Throw Island all year long. He had grown up here, in the house next to Nanny's; the same house his dad, Walter, spent his life in. I don't remember ever meeting Xavier, he was just always around. As soon as we arrived at Nanny's for the summer, he would ride up on his bike and the two of us would take off.

We were best friends until we were more and then we were nothing.

Tippenham, the southern town on Stone's Throw, has one main long road where the businesses are. There's the bike shop, a candy store, a book store, the café, a fancy restaurant that my parents never took us to, a few bars, and a small market where you could buy anything from groceries to fishing bait. In the ten years since we had been there, not a lot had changed. Some of the stores had different names, some were empty, and some were gone, including, I noticed, the book store.

The five of us walked our bikes down the street, one of The Ashleys saying how cute everything was, one trying to get gum off the bottom of her shoe, and the other talking Lauren's ear off.

Our rental cottage was on the other side of the island, farther out then Nanny's house had been. It was one of about a dozen small two-bedroom standalone rentals. Normally they'd be way out of our price range, but since we were here before Memorial Day, we were paying half price.

Despite my nerves, I walked my bike past the few storefronts and added my bike to the bike rack out front. No one here even bothered to lock them up. Everyone just trusted each other.

This island was from another time and I didn't know if I was ready to go back.

ACKNOWLEDGMENTS

It takes a ship of people to create a book, and I'm blessed with the best ship ever.

Thank you to all my writing captains, especially Julia Koty, who always makes sure I treat myself and my stories as a priority. Keep that compass handy, Julia; I would be lost at sea with out you!

Thank you to my Stone's Throw Island crew, Samantha Mayson and Luna Freeman, who jumped on board the moment I said, "You know what would be fun? ..." And Antony Charles hasn't walked the plank yet. I have faith he'll soon call, "Land-ho!" and dock at Stone's Throw.

Thank you to Kristen Wixted who supports everything I dream up, even when those dreams pull me away from our shared seaward adventures.

Thank you to my family—my lighthouse keepers—who always shine the way home.

And thank you to all the indie authors who share their sea of knowledge, octants, and lodestones to those who sail behind.

A high tide raises all boats.
Parker Rose

ABOUT THE AUTHOR

Parker Rose is an emerging author of small town romance. She lives in New England with her bunnies, her cats, her first mate, and three second mates. She loves exploring love, friendship, and one's true north, and occasionally consults her Magic Eight Ball for help with the biggest life questions.

Become a Stone's Throw Island VIP and receive exclusive stories from Parker by signing up at stonesthrowisland.com

facebook.com/AuthorParkerRose

Made in the USA
Columbia, SC
20 December 2022